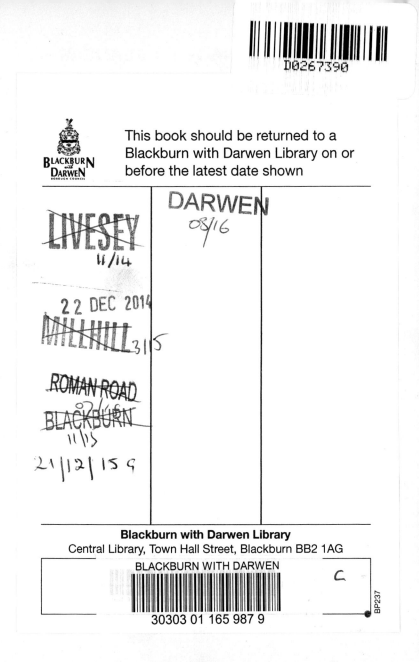

BLOOD LINES

Post-war midwife Maudie Rouse has her hands full tending to the pregnant, sick and injured villagers of Llandyfan, acting as their counsellor, and preparing for changes as the NHS comes into existence — including the possibility of being forced to move away from the people and the job she loves. The call of duty is never far away, even when she tries to steal a private moment with Constable Dick Bryant. Then a fortune-teller is found murdered at the village fête, and Maudie and Dick team up to search for answers . . .

Books by Catriona McCuaig
in the Linford Mystery Library:

THE MIDWIFE AND THE MURDER

CATRIONA McCUAIG

◆

BLOOD LINES

A Midwife Maudie Rouse mystery

Complete and Unabridged

LINFORD
Leicester

First published in Great Britain

First Linford Edition
published 2014

A catalogue record for this book is available
from the British Library.

01165 9879

ISBN 978–1–4448–2087–4

Published by
F. A. Thorpe (Publishing)
Anstey, Leicestershire

Set by Words & Graphics Ltd.
Anstey, Leicestershire
Printed and bound in Great Britain by
T. J. International Ltd., Padstow, Cornwall

This book is printed on acid-free paper

1

'Cuckoo!' Maudie Rouse said to herself. 'Absolutely cuckoo!' She leaned back in her swivel chair, trying to make sense of what had just happened. A woman had come to Maudie's tiny office in the parish hall, saying that she was new in Llandyfan and would like to register with her.

Maudie judged the woman to be in her fifties, perhaps a little older. Dressed in a washed-out grey cardigan and a droopy tweed skirt, she looked as if she had given up the struggle to maintain a youthful appearance. Perhaps that was unfair, however. Clothing was still rationed in England, despite the fact that the war had been over for three years; people still had to follow the make do and mend rule.

'I'm the local midwife,' Maudie explained. 'It's not me you have to register with, but Dr Mallory over at Midvale. If you'd like to give me your details I'll pass them on to him, unless of course you have any health concerns at present. I'm informed that we'll be getting a new doctor soon, and you may wish to transfer to his list then.'

'But wouldn't this Dr Mallory mind if I did that?' the woman asked.

'Oh, I expect he'll be retiring soon,' Maudie assured her. 'Or I should say, going back into retirement. He's well up in his eighties, poor man. He was hauled back into practice when the war broke out. Now then, may I have your name?'

'Blythe. I'm Myrtle Blythe.'

'Address?'

'I'm staying at the Royal Oak for the moment. That is, until I can find somewhere more permanent.'

'And good luck with that,' Maudie thought. So many people had been made homeless after the bombing that the building of new housing could not keep pace with the demand, and materials to maintain existing structures were practically unavailable.

'I'm looking for work,' the woman went on. 'I don't suppose I could be of assistance in your line?'

'Are you a midwife, then?' Maudie asked. 'Or a trained nurse, perhaps?'

'Not exactly, but I do know a lot about babies and childbirth. I've had ten of my own, you see.'

'Ten children!' Maudie's glance went to the ring finger on the woman's left hand. It was bare. Oh, well, perhaps she was a widow. 'Perhaps I should jot down their dates of birth, just to have them on file,' she said.

Myrtle Blythe screwed up her face in an effort to remember. 'Well, as far as I know, my first was Henry. He was born in 1536, and named after the king, of course.'

'What!' That must have been a slip of the tongue. 'Don't you mean 1936, Mrs Blythe?'

'Of course not. It was King George on the throne then, wasn't it? And it's *Miss* Blythe, thank you very much! Yes, I remember it well. That was the year they lopped Anne Boleyn's head off. Not likely to forget that, are we?'

'I suppose not,' Maudie said. The woman was obviously dotty, so it was best to let her ramble on. Who knew what she might be capable of if she was upset in any way? Although she didn't seem to be the violent type, it would be best to notify Dr Mallory as soon as she had gone, just in case. And it wouldn't hurt to notify the local constable, Dick Bryant, that he had a mental case on his patch.

Maudie had just hung up the phone after a confused conversation with Dr Mallory's receptionist, when she heard footsteps crossing the floor of the main hall. She stiffened. Her office was a small space partitioned off from the parish hall and it had only one door. There was no means of escape if she were to be trapped in here by a crazy person.

'Oh, it's you,' she said in some relief when she saw the vicar's wife approaching.

'And hello to you, too,' her friend said tartly.

'Sorry, Mrs Blunt; I didn't mean it the way it sounded. I've just had the most peculiar experience with a new patient. She seems to think she's had ten children, all born in a four-hundred-year period.'

'Oh, you mean that Miss Blythe,' Mrs Blunt replied. 'I saw her leaving when I was crossing the churchyard. Don't worry, Nurse. I'm sure she's not dangerous. She's a believer in reincarnation, that's all. She appears to be sane in every other way. Apparently she's had sessions with a hypnotist chap who deals in regression, as he calls it. According to her he has taken her back to various past lives, during which no doubt she gave birth to those babies she mentioned.'

'Well, I never did! Do you believe in that sort of stuff, then?'

'I understand that some Eastern religions do, but my husband certainly doesn't. What I find interesting is that in each of her so-called previous existences, she was just an ordinary person. Usually you hear of people claiming to be Marie Antoinette or somebody glamorous like that. It stands to reason that if there *was* such a thing as reincarnation, most of us would have been peasants. In any age the nobility were part of a very small group at the top.'

'There's no chance of my having been

Cleopatra, then,' Maudie said, grinning.

Mrs Blunt laughed. 'Florence Nightingale, perhaps? Now, the reason I came over here was to tell you we've received word of that new doctor we've been hoping for. His name is Donald Dean and he's in his early thirties, I believe.'

'Married?'

'I don't think so. He'll be joining Dr Mallory's practice, but our hope is that he'll make Llandyfan his home. That should spread the workload a little more fairly, and give you the chance to concentrate solely on your maternity cases.'

'And about time, too!' Although Maudie was a qualified midwife, it had been necessary for her to take on extra nursing duties during the war. The nearest district nurse was stationed ten miles away at Brookfield, and Dr Mallory was even further away at Midvale. With so many medical and nursing personnel serving with the armed forces, or trying to keep things together in the cities while the bombing was at its height, country nurses had been run off their feet because of staff shortages. Places like Llandyfan, a picturesque village close to the Welsh border, had been particularly hard-hit.

Maudie stood up and stretched. 'Here's to 1948, then! May it be better than 1947 was.'

'It could hardly be worse,' Mrs Blunt said.

'Do you mean the weather, or the murder?' Maudie wondered.

'Both, I suppose.'

January of that year had brought with it the coldest winter in living memory, with one snowstorm after another. Coal was in short supply, and of course none of the cottages possessed central heating. Not that it would have made any difference if they had, because of frequent power cuts. At times the huge snow drifts had made it impossible for Maudie to visit patients on her trusty bicycle, and in one case she'd had to take an expectant mother into her own cottage a week before her due date, just in case the poor woman might be stranded when her time came.

When spring finally arrived they had to

face flooding as the snow melted. On one never-to-be forgotten occasion, Maudie had been conveyed to a patient's home in a leaky rowboat after the nearby river had burst its banks.

'And when all that was behind us we had the murder,' Mrs Blunt said, as if Maudie needed reminding. She'd been taking a shortcut through some woods when she'd come across the victim, a man who had been garroted.[1] The killer had eventually been caught and hanged, but not before he'd attacked Maudie herself.

'I was really dreading this past winter because I thought it might be more of the same,' Maudie said, trying to change the subject. 'It wasn't too bad, though, was it?'

'And I think it's safe to say that spring is here,' Mrs Blunt agreed. 'Have you seen all my crocuses at the rectory? I do love those purple-and-white striped ones. And I meant to tell you that we'll be having a parish fête this summer, for the

---

[1] See *The Midwife and the Murder* by Catriona McCuaig.

first time since before the war. That should cheer everybody up.'

'Here's to a happy year, with absolutely no murders!' Maudie said.

2

'Hello, Dick! What brings you here?' Maudie looked up from her case notes to see her friend framed in the doorway. Constable Dick Bryant was officially stationed at Midvale, but his duties took him all over the district. Maudie had come to know him in nineteen forty-seven when they had been investigating the murder of a visitor to the area, and since then they had shared a number of happy outings.

'Shoplifting,' he replied. 'Mrs Hatch at the shop has noticed things going missing lately. The problem is that when she's attending to people at the post office counter, she can't keep an eye on what's going on behind the shelves.'

'I expect it's school children, don't you think?'

Bryant shook his head. 'I'm not so sure. A child might snatch a chocolate bar or a tube of wine gums and hide them in his pocket, but other items are going as well. Things like tins of Spam or corned beef. You'd think the culprit must be someone with a shopping basket. If a youngster tried to conceal something like that up his jumper he'd be noticed.'

'Perhaps not, if Mrs Hatch was making out a postal order at the time,' Maudie mused. 'So what do you mean to do?'

Bryant scratched his head. 'Mrs Hatch wants me to dust for fingerprints, but a fat lot of good that would be. Shops are a mass of fingerprints, what with people picking up tins to read the label and putting them back down, having changed their minds. I've suggested to Mrs Hatch that she gets a glass case made for the chocolate bars and sherbet dabs so that people can see what's on offer without being able to pick them up. The other sweets are safe enough, kept in those big jars with lids on.'

'And does Mrs Hatch have no clue at all who might be responsible?'

Bryant grinned. 'Only that it's somebody who is partial to Fry's peppermint bars! Unless there are actually two or more thieves: say a kiddie who takes chocolate, and some housewife feathering her nest.'

'It's this beastly rationing,' Maudie said. 'People are so sick and tired of everything being in such short supply. I'm sure that if the day ever comes when they take food and luxuries off the ration, there will be less temptation to take things that don't belong to them.'

'I wish I had your faith in human nature,' Bryant said.

'Ah, well, I expect you've seen it all,' Maudie said. 'By the way, I meant to tell you; we've got a very odd woman here. A newcomer, staying at the Royal Oak.'

'Odd? In what way?'

'Listen to this, Dick. She swanned in here, telling me she'd given birth to ten children.'

'So what? My gran had fifteen, and managed to raise eleven of them.'

'Ah, but did she have them all at once?'

Bryant stared at Maudie, puzzled. 'Of course she didn't. There was one set of twins, but nobody has fifteen all at once. Although now I come to think of it, my uncle's sheepdog had fourteen pups all in one litter.'

'I'm putting this badly,' Maudie told him. 'This Miss Blythe claims to have had children in previous lives, starting with a boy born in the time of Henry VIII. According to what she told Mrs Blunt, she'd had some mad scheme of selling the child to Anne Boleyn, who could pass it off as her own child, thereby meeting the king's need for a son and heir. Unfortunately poor old Anne lost her head on the block before they could work out the details.'

Bryant looked blank. Maudie sighed. Obviously he'd been standing behind the door when the history lessons were given out, she thought. Having no wish to make him feel small, she changed tactics. 'Let me put it this way, Dick. This woman believes she's been on earth in several previous existences. Some quack has convinced her to the point where she believes she can recall a lot of the details, including the births of children.'

'Oh, yes?'

'But I can't decide whether she's a

harmless eccentric or completely bats. Can you understand what I'm saying? If it's the latter, she'll want watching. Who knows what she might get up to?'

'Like nicking tins of corned beef, you mean?'

Maudie stared at him suspiciously, but he was smirking. 'What's the point of giving you useful information if all you can do is to take the mickey, Dick Bryant?'

'I just believe in keeping an open mind, Nurse. This woman isn't necessarily deranged. She might have a genuine belief in reincarnation, as many Asians do. Just because she doesn't subscribe to everyday Church of England beliefs, we mustn't label her as a loony.'

'That's just it,' Maudie said, exasperated. 'She does call herself C of E. She attends St John's, for goodness sake! That's what makes me think that she's fallen into the hands of some charlatan who preys on lonely women. You can bet your police-issue boots that he doesn't do it for nothing. And who knows what dangerous ideas he may have put into her mind?'

'It's a free country, Maudie.' Dick Bryant spoke gently. 'Isn't that what we were fighting for — the freedom to believe in our own ideas, and to live as we think fit, within the law?'

'I suppose so, but I'm not comfortable with it and it won't surprise me at all if having Miss Myrtle Blythe in the village leads to trouble. And when that happens, don't you dare say I didn't warn you!'

As if on cue, the outer door banged and a man lunged into the hall, holding a squalling infant at some distance from his body. Bryant wrinkled his nose at the smell emanating from the child.

'I think I'll, er . . . ' he began, but the man moved in front of him to stop him leaving.

'It's you I want, Constable!' he roared. 'The woman at the shop told me you were here.'

Wordlessly, Maudie reached up to a high shelf for a clean towelling nappy, which she spread out on her desk before reaching for the child. The fretful wailing stopped and the little boy favoured her with a toothless smile.

'It's my wife!' the man snapped. 'She's run off somewhere and I want her found!' He turned to Maudie, scowling. 'I blame you for this, Nurse! If you hadn't pampered her so much she'd have pulled herself together by now!'

Maudie learned towards Dick. 'Post-partum depression,' she murmured out of the side of her mouth.

He nodded. 'And your name is, sir?'

'Allen. Paul Allen.'

'And what makes you think she's run off, sir? Perhaps she's just slipped round to see a neighbour?'

'Then why wouldn't she take Clark with her?' the man sneered.

Maudie was horrified. 'You don't mean to tell me she left the baby home alone, Mr Allen?'

'No, of course not. I got home from work and went straight upstairs to have a bit of a wash. Clarice was dithering around in the kitchen and Clark here was in his pram. When I came back down there was no sign of any tea on the table so I went to the kitchen to tell her to get moving. That's when I found her note.'

16

'She left a note? May I see it, sir?'

'I left it on the kitchen table. All it said was, 'I must get out of here. It's your turn now.' What did she mean by that, hey? I do my bit, going out to work to make a living for us all. Clarice has the best of it. She can stay at home all day with nothing to do but please herself. No difficult bosses to please. No pressure of work in a busy office. Oh, no! But when I get home after a brute of a day, what do I find? A messy house, a howling infant and no meal in sight. This was not what I expected when I agreed to take her on, Constable; I can tell you that!'

Cradling little Clark in her arms, Maudie forced herself to keep quiet. She'd had dealings with this man before, and it wouldn't help if she lost her temper now. She waited to see what Bryant might do.

'How long were you at home before coming to see me, sir?'

'As I said, I had a wash, and then I found her gone. Let's say I was upstairs for about ten, fifteen minutes. Then I came down, found her gone, and rushed over here at once.'

'Without stopping to change that child's nappy?' Maudie couldn't resist saying. The look he gave her conveyed exactly what he thought of that suggestion.

'And Mrs Allen was at home when you first arrived, sir?'

'I've said so, haven't I? Look, man, why are we wasting time standing here? Clarice has to be found right away. Can't you understand that?'

'Yes, sir, of course. Now then, where do you think she might have gone? Have you checked the village shop in case she's gone to buy something for your tea? Or what about women friends? Might she have popped round to see one of them?'

Allen glared at Bryant. 'She can't have gone shopping because she didn't come to me for money. As for friends, she doesn't have any.'

Bryant and Maudie exchanged looks. 'Have you any reason to believe she may try to do away with herself?' Bryant asked carefully.

3

The two men left, leaving the baby with Maudie, without so much as a by-your-leave. That was typical of Paul Allen, she thought. He had fixed ideas about a woman's place in the world where, of course, men were meant to rule.

Clarice Allen had been overtaken by post-partum depression after their little boy was born, and Maudie had done all she could to encourage the young woman to adjust to her new circumstances. On getting married Clarice had left a job where she had lively company all day, and a wage packet that was hers to spend as she wished. She had fallen pregnant soon after her wedding day and had given birth within the year. While hormonal changes and sleep deprivation might be to blame for the depression, Maudie could well understand how the abrupt changes in the girl's lifestyle only added to her burden.

She had tried to explain this to the husband, but he had only brushed this off as women's nonsense. In many ways Maudie approved of the division of labour in a traditional marriage. When a man went out to work to provide for his family, it was up to his wife to play her part by providing him with a comfortable home. But there had to be sympathy and understanding on both sides. How degrading it must be to have to go to one's husband, cap in hand, to wait while he doled out the money she needed to go shopping! And, from what Maudie knew of Paul Allen, he probably made his wife account for every penny she'd spent, expecting to be given the change.

Maudie had recently set up a mother-and-baby group, where women could relieve the tedium of spending all day at home, with only demanding infants for company. She'd had women like Mrs Allen in mind when planning this, yet Clarice had never shown her face at these get-togethers. Had her husband forbidden her to attend? Or did she lack the motivation because she was depressed?

Maudie had suggested a visit to Dr Mallory, who might be able to prescribe something to alleviate the situation. Paul Allen had said it wasn't necessary. Visits to the doctor cost money. Maudie looked forward to the summer of 1948, when the new National Health Service would come into effect. Visits to the doctor would be free, as would medicine obtained on prescription, and dental care. However, the new scheme didn't mean that the likes of Paul Allen would see the light.

Baby Clark wriggled in her arms. 'We'd better go and look for your mummy, hadn't we,' she said, planting a kiss on top of his silky hair. The baby gurgled. 'Now then, my boy; where do you think mummy could have gone? We'll go and have a look, shall we? We'd better see if you need changing again first.' She patted his knitted pilch and found it dry.

'Where would I go if I wanted to get away from it all?' Maudie wondered aloud. Well, in her case she'd curl up in bed with a cup of tea and a mystery novel, but Clarice hadn't done that. When she was feeling frayed Maudie enjoyed a stroll down along the riverbank, but she expected that the two men would have already thought of that, in case Clarice entertained thoughts of doing away with herself.

'The church, then,' Maudie told young Clark. 'It's right next door, so we may as well start there.' She had no idea whether his mother was a religious person, but in times of difficulty people seemed to gravitate to the old Norman building with its aura of serenity. There was something about the idea that generations of people had brought their problems here that brought comfort to the troubled mind.

Outside the parish hall Maudie looked around for Clark's pram, but it was nowhere to be seen. Allen must have scooped the child up in his arms and run all the way to find the constable without thinking. Perhaps that was a sign that he cared about his wife after all.

Maudie slipped into the church by the vestry door, breathing a sigh of relief when she noticed Clarice sitting in a pew in the lady chapel. Clarice was not alone. Miss Blythe was sitting beside her, apparently giving her an earnest lecture, to which the young woman was responding by nodding and smiling. Smiling was good, thought Maudie, but she had to nip this in the bud. Moving swiftly on her crêpe-soled shoes, she slipped into the pew so that Clarice was trapped between the two older women.

'I'll be off, then,' Miss Blythe announced, looking down her long nose at Maudie. 'I must say it's a shame if one can't have a quiet conversation in church without being interrupted by those who scoff and sneer.' She stood up abruptly and stalked towards the altar. Recognizing his mother, baby Clark reached up his arms to her. Clarice took him from Maudie, murmuring endearments.

'Let's go and sit outside in the sun, shall we?' Maudie suggested, and was relieved when the girl obediently stood up and followed. Maudie led the way to a wooden bench, conveniently located in front of an ancient yew tree, and they sat down with the baby on the grass nearby.

'He sat up all on his own for the first time this morning,' Clarice said proudly.

'That's quite advanced for his age, isn't it, Nurse?'

'All babies progress at their own speed,' Maudie said tactfully, 'but yes, Clark is doing very well. You haven't been worried about him, have you, Mrs Allen?'

Clarice shrugged. 'I suppose you wonder what I'm doing here, when I should be at home putting my husband's meal on the table. Well, I couldn't help it. I just felt the need to get out of the house for a while, just to have a few minutes to myself. I left Clark with Paul so he'd see what it's like having to keep an eye on a baby all round the clock. He's never taken much interest in his son, you know. He says that's women's work. Just for once I wanted him to feel responsible.'

'Which is why he brought Clark and his dirty nappy to me, I suppose.'

'Did he really, Nurse? You mean he brought Clark to you and went back home without him?'

Honest forced Maudie to explain. 'He's out searching for you, my dear. He's taken the constable with him.'

Clarice's face turned white. 'I hope

Paul doesn't think I've done something silly,' she murmured. 'I've been feeling low, but I'd never do a thing like that, Nurse. Not when Clark here is depending on me. Yes, I did run out while Paul was upstairs, but I thought the baby would be all right with him.'

'I quite understand,' Maudie assured her. 'We all need to get away on our own once in a while. And I always find St John's a peaceful place, don't you?'

'I met that woman you saw me with there,' Clarice said. 'She came and sat down beside me and started to talk. I was feeling so sorry for myself, but after she told me how much she'd suffered it made me feel ashamed. Compared with her I've really nothing to complain about.'

'Oh?' Maudie said, wondering what was coming next. 'She died twice, you know, Nurse,' Clarice went on. 'Can you imagine something so awful? I suppose they had to do artificial respiration on her or something to bring her round. I thought I was hard done by with that long labour I had, but she must have suffered so much more.'

'Um,' Maudie said, wondering if she should explain Myrtle Blythe's belief that she had died in childbirth — twice — in her so-called past lives. 'I hope she didn't upset you with her stories?'

'Now you mention it, Nurse, it has made me wonder if I might die next time.'

'Next time? Are you pregnant, Mrs Allen?'

The colour returned to the young woman's cheeks. 'No, but Paul thinks it's time I was. We don't want Clark to be an only child, and Paul says if the next one is to be a proper playmate for Clark, we need to get started soon. Only the way I'm feeling, I don't feel like — you know, Nurse, relations — and he keeps demanding his rights, as he calls them, and everything is just such a mess!' She broke into tears, wiping her cheeks on the sleeve of her striped blouse.

Paul says! Paul says! Maudie thought. It was certainly not her place to come between husband and wife in such matters, but oh, how she longed to give Paul Allen a good swift kick in the seat of the pants! 'Women very rarely die in childbirth in this day and age,' she said firmly. 'And if and when you do give birth again, I shall be here to see that you do not. You can count on me, my dear.'

Clarice gave her a grateful smile.

4

Maudie looked up from her notes to find a tall, blond-haired man framed in the doorway of her tiny office. He had piercing blue eyes and a fair complexion. Some lucky woman had nabbed this handsome man as the father of her child and if the baby took after him, it was bound to be good-looking, whether male or female.

'Can I help you?' she asked, giving him her best smile. 'Would you like to sit down while I make a note of your details?'

'There is hardly room for both of us in this cubbyhole,' he snapped, looking around disparagingly. 'As for my details, as you call them, I happen to be Dr Dean!'

Oops! 'How do you do, Doctor,' Maudie said, resisting the urge to leap to her feet. In a hospital setting she might have considered bowing and scraping, but out here they were colleagues on an equal footing. 'I'm the midwife, Nurse Rouse.'

'I hardly thought you could be anyone else,' he replied, 'unless you are in the habit of letting all and sundry meddle with your patients' case notes.' Had he accompanied this remark with a smile, the words would have seemed innocuous, but his grim expression held more than a hint of censure. What was the matter with the man? Her neat uniform proclaimed her as a nurse, and he had no reason to think that she was inefficient where her work was concerned.

She managed to avoid making a tart remark. There was no point in antagonizing the man before they'd even got to know each other; after all, she would have to work with the man. 'We heard you were coming, Doctor. You've joined Dr Mallory's practice, have you?'

'I've bought into it, yes,' he corrected her. 'One has to start somewhere, of course, but it can hardly be a partnership when the man is about to go back into retirement. This is merely a matter of convenience, to enable me to take over the patients on his list.'

'Of course,' Maudie murmured. 'And you'll be working out of his surgery, I suppose.'

'Hardly! The man sees people in his own home. Hardly hygienic, I would have thought, but there you are. The war forced all of us to make concessions to the circumstances. I shall demand that other, more suitable premises be found for me.'

'I see.'

'I had hoped that this place would do, but I can see now that it would be quite impossible. Perhaps the Reverend Blunt will see to it that the parish hall is adapted for me. I shall need consulting rooms, of course, and storage facilities, and extra lavatories and a sluice room.'

'I see,' Maudie repeated, aware of the need to go carefully. And what was supposed to happen to all the people who used the parish hall for recreational purposes? The Scouts, Guides, Cubs and Brownies all met here, as did the Women's Institute and the Mothers' Union. She wouldn't like to be present when Dr Dean and the Reverend Blunt went ten rounds together to sort this one out. On the other hand, it might be rather fun to be a fly on the wall when it happened. Mr Blunt was what was known as a muscular Christian. He was a good and gentle man and a faithful leader of his flock, but when it came to standing up for his principles he was as immoveable as the Rock of Gibraltar.

Dismissing the thought of the fight to come, she smiled nervously at the doctor, who was still on his feet, standing to attention with his arms folded. She attempted to come up with something harmless to say, and that was where she made her mistake. 'But you will be making Midvale your headquarters, won't you? I mean, the biggest concentration of our patients is there.'

He shrugged. 'The council have made it quite clear that they want me stationed in the Llandyfan district; not that it matters much to me, when I have a car. If they can provide me with the facilities I need I can foresee no difficulty there.'

Maudie nodded glumly. The idea of

sitting in her cubbyhole, as he called it, while all the noisy renovations went on nearby, was a bit much to take. Perhaps she could temporarily see patients in the front room of her cottage.

As if he had read her thoughts, he said, 'There is, of course, the question of accommodation. Perhaps we can take a look at your cottage now?'

'I beg your pardon?' Maudie was appalled. Surely she wasn't expected to take in a lodger? And certainly not one of the opposite sex! Why, her reputation would be in tatters as soon as the Mothers' Union got to hear about that! 'It's really quite cramped,' she stammered. 'There isn't room for two people. I can't imagine how people managed in the days when couples had to bring up a large family in a couple of rooms.'

'I'm not married, Nurse. I'm sure it will do for me, just until something more suitable comes along. Now, can we go? My time is valuable, even if yours is not.'

'There must be some mistake, Dr Dean. I have no plans to leave my cottage. It suits me very well and I'm quite settled there.'

'But you won't be needing it for much longer, will you, Nurse? You'll be moving on. Now, I must insist that we go at once, unless you wish to give me the key and furnish me with directions to enable me to find it for myself.'

Maudie's mouth dropped open. All right, she'd show the beastly chap around her cottage, but he needn't think he was taking it over. There was a major misunderstanding here somewhere that would have to be sorted out. As they walked down the lane she realized that she'd left the place in a bit of a mess. Her breakfast dishes had been washed, but left to drain dry beside the sink. Her bed had been left unmade. It had been a firm rule in her training hospital that beds were left to air for several hours before being made up again; she had followed this practice ever since. Her spare pair of stockings had been rinsed through and were hanging in the scullery to dry, along with a sturdy pair of knickers; scarcely a sight to gladden the eyes of this fashion plate who possessed an icicle in place of a heart. And what about the living room? She had left her knitting and several mystery novels lying about, and what was wrong with that? That was the beauty of living alone. You could please yourself in your own surroundings.

Maudie opened the door, which led straight into the living room. She usually came and went by the back door, but there was no way she intended to subject Dr Dean to the sight of her darned stockings and patched knickers, steadily dripping water onto the stone floor of the scullery. At her appearance a ginger shape arose from her armchair, yawning and stretching.

'You have a cat in here!' the doctor said, glaring at poor Perkin, who strolled over to wrap himself around the visitor's legs.

'He's not mine. He's the rectory cat, actually.' Maudie realized now that she'd forgotten to close the larder window and the animal must have entered that way, no doubt hoping to find some delicacy on the marble slab where she kept her perishables cold. Please don't let him have finished off my bacon ration, she prayed.

'Get off, you brute!' The wretched man shook his leg to get rid of the cat, who yowled and leapt onto the sideboard. 'Just look at my trousers, you silly woman! Covered in hair! I trust you'll give this place a thorough cleaning before I move in here. Now then, what's upstairs? I suppose there's a bathroom and I won't be expected to wash in a tin tub in a lean-to somewhere.'

'Oh, there is a proper bath tub,' Maudie told him through gritted teeth. And I'd like to drown you in it, she thought, although she didn't say it aloud. Last year there had been a murder in Llandyfan and she felt quite sure that if this man stayed on for any length of time there would be a second one in due course. She sighed, admitting to herself that this was a mere fantasy. However, one thing was certain: once the locals came to know him it would not be long before they demanded that he be sent back to where he came from. Country folk were slow to anger, but when roused they could become filled with righteous indignation, and then they would stand firm. This was the spirit that had won the war against the tyrant Hitler!

5

Maudie telephoned to Dick Bryant at the Midvale police station. It was the first time she had ever done such a thing on purely personal business, but she was desperately in need of someone in a semi-official capacity to help her sort this out.

'Is there any chance you could come over?' she pleaded. 'Everything is falling to pieces here and if I don't have anyone to talk to about it I think I'll go mad!'

'Fear not,' he joked. 'Sir Galahad will be with you in fifteen minutes.'

'You can't get here that fast,' Maudie said.

'I can if I put the siren on. I shall bring my trusty sword, ready to do battle with the fearsome dragon on my lady's behalf.'

'Fool,' she told him, but there was affection in her voice. It was closer to half an hour before he appeared, by which time Maudie felt ready to weep.

'Would you like to go somewhere?' he asked, looking at her with concern in his brown eyes.

'Better not. I'm supposed to be on duty. People have to know where to find me so I mustn't go far from a telephone in working hours.'

'Same here, actually. Sarge is on the warpath and I'd rather not do anything to annoy him.'

'I hope I haven't landed you in trouble.'

'It's all right. He thinks I'm coming here to talk to Mrs Hatch. Some of her goods have gone missing again. Sardines in tomato sauce, if you please. Oh, and three boxes of Swan Vestas.'

'I don't like the sound of that,' Maudie said. Why would anyone steal matches, unless they mean to get up to mischief?

'Maudie Rouse, is that why you dragged me all the way over here — to start fretting about arsonists? Just sit down and tell me what's happened, will you?' Haltingly, Maudie recounted her experience with Dr Dean. 'It sounds to me as if the man has a high opinion of himself,' Dick said, when she finally ran out of steam. 'Well, you've met doctors like him before, old girl, and lived to tell the tale. My advice is to ignore the fellow and just get on with the job.'

'That's the problem,' she cried. 'I may not have a job to get on with! He implies that I'm not needed here anymore. Why else would he expect to move into my cottage? *My* cottage, Dick! I pay the rent! Can I be forced to move? And with this new health scheme coming into play, can I be made to go?'

'That's something you'll have to find out. Let's suppose for a minute that it's true. Can the powers that be transfer you to another district over your objections? If they made you redundant here, would you be responsible for finding another position for yourself?'

'If they sack me, you mean?' Maudie said, her face the picture of misery. 'What sort of reference would they give me, do you think?'

'An excellent one, of course. You've done wonders here, Maudie, and don't let anyone tell you otherwise, least of all that Dr Dean.'

'I don't want to leave!' Maudie howled. 'I like Llandyfan, I love my job, and my ladies depend on me. I'm settled here and I don't want to start all over again somewhere else. What am I going to do, Dick? Just what am I going to do?'

Dick leapt up and took her into his arms, patting her on the back while she sobbed into his shoulder. 'You could always marry me,' he told her.

Maudie laughed through her tears. 'Don't be so silly,' she said. She did not see the hurt on his face. She pulled away from him then, fumbling for her handkerchief. He was about to offer her one of his own when they heard a cough behind them. They sprang apart at the sight of the vicar.

'I'm so sorry to intrude,' he said carefully, 'but you're wanted, Constable. There has been an occurrence of what sounds to me like attempted murder, down by the river. A small boy on a bicycle brought the news just moments ago, and luckily I caught a glimpse of you coming here when I was weeding the garden. The child will take you to the scene. And Nurse, I think that perhaps you had better accompany them.'

Maudie scrambled into the police car beside Dick. The small boy, his eyes bright with excitement, helped Dick to load his bicycle into the boot before squeezing in beside Maudie.

'Do you know what happened?' she asked.

The child nodded. 'Yes, miss. This lady fell in the river and I think she drowned.'

Maudie felt sick. She very much hoped that it wasn't Clarice Allen who had decided to put an end to herself.

'Did anyone try to help this lady?' Dick asked. The boy nodded. 'Yes, sir. Some men pulled her out and told me to get help. They were doing that thing you taught the Scouts how do. Official desperation, it's called. My brother knows how to do it. He's a Scout, he is.'

'Artificial respiration,' Maudie murmured, too upset to laugh.

'That's what I said, miss.'

'We're coming to the river now,' Dick

observed. 'Where exactly did the incident take place?'

'Up there by the old boathouse, sir. You can drive right in because the gravel road ends there.'

Sure enough, they soon saw a small group of people on the riverbank. A woman in soaking garments was sitting on the grass with her back against the trunk of an elm tree, peevishly refusing a blanket offered to her by a bystander. With a sinking feeling, Maudie recognized her as Myrtle Blythe. She resolved to keep quiet and let Dick do his job unless, of course, she was required to give nursing help to the victim.

'I'm quite all right now!' the woman insisted. 'Please take me to the Royal Oak where I can get into dry clothes!'

'What exactly happened here?' Bryant asked.

An older man, clutching the lead of a shaggy brown dog, answered importantly. 'I'm out walking Fergus here when I hears a commotion. Coming on the scene, I sees these chaps pulling that lady out of the water. I didn't think she was breathing, so I started artificial respiration. I learned that in the Home Guard during the war. And then she come to, all of a sudden.'

'Right,' Bryant said. 'I'll make a note of your names and addresses now because I'll need to speak to you all later. First things first: we must take the lady home. Nurse?'

Maudie came forward at once. 'It's me, Miss Blythe. Nurse Rouse. You're quite safe now, but you must let me put this blanket around you. We don't want you catching pneumonia! Are you able to walk to the car, do you think? Here, take my arm.' Muttering under her breath, Miss Blythe allowed Maudie to settle her in the car, while Dick retrieved the small bicycle from the boot. The boy would have a fine story to tell his friends now.

'I won't bother you just now, madam,' Dick said as he started up the car, 'but I shall have to take your statement later. Don't you worry about that; it's just a routine procedure. You were walking by the river, lost your footing and slipped into the water. Isn't that so?'

Miss Blythe cowered in her seat, putting up a hand to push back strands of wet hair from her forehead. 'Oh, no, Constable! I didn't slip. I was pushed!' Her voice rose. 'Someone tried to kill me!

6

Mrs Blunt was all agog to hear Maudie's story. 'I really shouldn't pry,' she said, 'only I do feel we are involved in a way. Harold heard about it from the young Price boy, and you happened to be with the constable when my husband rushed over to tell him what had happened. How is the poor woman this morning? Harold is wondering if he should make a pastoral visit, but we have no wish to intrude if she's feeling a bit frail.'

'I nipped over to the pub at breakfast time,' Maudie said. 'Physically, she seems to have recovered, but I'm not so sure about her mental state.'

'Oh?'

'She insists that she didn't just have an unfortunate accident, but was pushed. She says that someone tried to kill her.'

'Surely not!'

'Ah, but wait for it. She says it was her husband.'

'What? Isn't she a maiden lady?'

'So far as we know. But it's this business of her past lives, you see. Obviously if she really did go through previous existences — and I think that's all a lot of hogwash, Mrs Blunt — then in each case she would have died eventually.'

'Of course.'

'So in her fantasy, or whatever it is, one of her husbands may have murdered her, and that's got her confused with what must have been an unlucky fall yesterday while she was strolling along the river-bank. The grass has been quite slippery after the rain.'

'And what does Dick think?'

'He's inclined to agree with me. He's spoken to the men who fished her out of the water, and they are quite adamant that there was nobody else about at the time. No evil strangers or jostling youths. Unfortunately they were out of sight when it happened, just around the corner, scraping down a boat. The first they were aware of anything wrong was when they heard a cry and a splash, and they came running. Then the Home Guard man joined them and they sent the Price child to look for Dick.'

'It does sound as though the poor soul is confused,' Mrs Blunt said. 'Shouldn't her people be notified? Surely she shouldn't be wandering about alone if she has dementia?'

'I did ask her if I could notify anyone of her accident, but apparently her only living relative is a sister in America. Besides, apart from this business of her past lives, so-called, she seems to know how many beans make five.'

'I can see the difficulty.'

'Yes, well, look at it from Dick's point of view. If she really was pushed, that's attempted murder or at least a vicious assault, and the police should be doing all they can to solve the crime. But if her mind is wandering, that would be a waste of manpower and they are busy enough as it is.'

'I do believe she should be assessed by a doctor,' Mrs Blunt said firmly. 'Have you reported this to Dr Dean?'

'Oh, him!' Maudie sniffed.

Her friend frowned. 'What's the matter,

Nurse? Don't you care for him? My impression of him is that he's a most efficient young man.'

'Oh, he's efficient, all right,' Maudie said bitterly. 'Like a tank going over a molehill. Believe me, if we'd set him up against Hitler the war would have been over a lot sooner.'

Mrs Blunt laughed. 'He can't be that bad, surely? Perhaps you'll change your opinion when you get to know him better.'

'I may not get the chance. He seems to think I'll be getting the sack, or at least be transferred out of the district. He's already planning to take over my cottage, although not before I give it a good clean from top to bottom! And no, I'm not exaggerating,' she added, seeing Mrs Blunt's sceptical look.

When she realized that Maudie had genuine concerns about her future, Mrs Blunt immediately swung into vicar's-wife mode. 'I shall speak to Harold,' she announced, 'and he will look into the situation. It may not be as bad as you think, Nurse. As I understand it, the provisions of this new Health Act don't really come into play until the summer, and even if there are a few new brooms running things at the top, I can't see that it would be in the best interests of the community to make such sweeping changes.'

'Do you know, I've been looking forward to the implementation of the health scheme,' Maudie replied. 'I thought we might get another nurse to attend to the daily needs of the community, while I'd be left free to get on with my midwifery.'

'And that may well come about. But it might be an idea to make contingency plans, just in case. Have you thought what you might do if it came to the crunch?'

Maudie shrugged. 'I haven't had time to think. This business with Miss Blythe put my own troubles out of my mind. I suppose I've been glad to coast along here, expecting I'd be in Llandyfan for the rest of my working life, as long as I didn't blot my copybook in some way. Now, I just don't know!'

Walking back to the parish hall,

swinging her arms, Maudie held her head high. She despised herself for going to pieces in front of Dick the day before. What had happened to the calm and practical woman who had brought so many mothers safely through the ordeal of childbirth? She was a woman in her forties, not a silly schoolgirl afraid to confess that she hadn't done her homework. 'Don't cross your bridges before you come to them,' she muttered, quoting her old granny, now long gone to her reward.

* * *

'There you are, Nurse! I thought you were never coming.' The wooden floor of the parish hall creaked as the woman came forward to meet Maudie.

'Good morning, Mrs Black. How can I help you?'

'It's not me that needs the help. It's my husband.'

'Oh, yes? Isn't he feeling well?'

'Oh, he's well enough, strutting around like a turkey cock on a dunghill. I want someone to talk to him; straighten out his thinking!'

'Perhaps the vicar . . . ' Maudie began.

'Oh, him! What we need is someone who'll give him the woman's point of view.'

'And this is about . . . ?'

'He wants to stop them getting wed, Nurse. Our Greta and young Matt. Time's getting on and that baby won't have a name unless we get on with it soon.'

'But surely weddings are a matter for the vicar,' Maudie pointed out, but Mrs Black refused to listen. Maudie found herself agreeing to visit the woman's home that evening, prepared to do battle.

She knew that young Greta Black was nearing her time because the young girl had been under Maudie's care since the beginning of her pregnancy. She was a flighty little madam who seemed to care about only two things: her boyfriend, a good-looking young garage mechanic named Matt, and the Hollywood stars whose progress she followed avidly. Maudie had visited the girl's bedroom and seen their pictures, clipped from magazines, that covered the walls. She was proud of the fact that she was named after a star from her mother's cinema-going days, Greta Garbo.

Far from taking flight when Greta's pregnancy was discovered, Matt was willing to marry the girl and settle down with her to bring up their baby. As Maudie knew only too well, many desperate parents would be thankful if the father of their grandchild agreed to accept responsibility, but not everyone was that fortunate.

Why, then, was Frank Black prepared to put a spanner in the works? She would have to meet with him to find out, and she hoped that she could make a useful contribution to the discussion. This was where a midwife was the ideal person for the job. There was much more to her craft than simply bringing a child safely into the world, although of course that was the most vital part of the process. She was also there to advise at all stages of the game, both before and after the confinement.

Maudie had to admit that she loved being involved in the lives of her patients. Being the keeper of their secrets made her feel that her existence on this earth was worthwhile, and who could wish for more?

7

Frank Black sat in a high-backed wooden armchair, giving the impression of a king seated on his throne. His wife was perched on the edge of a sagging sofa, struggling up once or twice to straighten an antimacassar or to move an object on the end table. Greta Black, heavily pregnant, lolled in an armchair and her young man stood behind her, wearing a hunted look on his face. Stealing a glance at him, Maudie wondered if she should offer him a remedy for his acne, but decided to leave that for another time.

Frank Black spoke. 'Well, Mother! You wanted me to stay in for this fool meeting, and here I am! So let's get on with it, shall we?'

His wife nodded her head in Maudie's direction. 'You tell him, Nurse!'

Maudie gulped. 'Well, I'm not sure it's my place to say anything, but . . . '

'Just get on with it, woman!' Frank

growled. 'I believe in calling a spade a spade, so you may as well say your piece.'

'Oh, Dad!' It was Greta who came to the rescue. 'Me and Matt want to get married, and you won't let us. Nurse is here to make you change your mind.'

'Perhaps we should listen to Mr Black's point of view,' Maudie put in hastily, seeing the man's complexion darken with rage. It would help nobody if he had a stroke on the spot. 'What are your reasons for refusing your consent to the marriage, Mr Black?'

'She's too young, that's what! Just seventeen and not a brain in her head! Marriage is for life. If she ties herself down now she'll regret it for the rest of her days. The law understands that, and that's why a girl need her father's say-so if she wants to get hitched before the age of twenty-one.'

'But think of the disgrace, Frank!' his wife blurted. 'Can't we at least give the child a name?'

'And what sort of name would that be, hey? The name of a nineteen-year old boy!'

Maudie looked from one to the other, framing her words with care. 'Quite aside from that, Mr Black, what would you like to see your daughter do? Like it or not, this baby is on its way. Just a few weeks from now it will be a live presence in this house. What will you do then?'

'That will be entirely up to you, Nurse.'

'Me?' Maudie squeaked. 'I don't know what you mean!'

'Then let me put it in simple language. You will come here to see the child safely into the world. Despite what you may be thinking, I do want the best for my girl. When it's born you'll take it away with you, that's all I'm asking.'

'And what do you expect me to do with the child, exactly?'

'You know more about these things than I do, woman. Deliver it to wherever babies go for adoption. It comes from good stock. Some childless couple will be glad of it.'

'If only life were so simple,' Maudie told him. 'It's more likely to end up in an orphanage. Those places are full of children who lost their parents in the war,

56

or were born as a result of wartime liaisons. Don't you realize that Britain has been sending unwanted children abroad for years, to Canada and Australia, to work on farms and the like? Is that what you want for your grandchild, Mr Black? Do you really want Greta to spend the rest of her life worrying over what has become of her firstborn child?'

'She should have thought of that before!' he grunted.

His wife made a little sound like the mew of a cat but he silenced her with a glare. 'I've said my piece, Nurse, and that's all I intend to say. I shall send for you when Greta needs your help, and in the meantime you can find out where to take the baby. Ask the vicar. The Church of England must have such places.'

Maudie rose to her feet. There was simply no point in arguing with the man. She made up her mind to call on Mrs Blunt on her way home. While she hoped and prayed that Frank Black might relent, she had to be prepared for any eventuality.

'What a shame,' Mrs Blunt murmured,

when Maudie had explained to her about the unhappy gathering she'd just been a part of. 'There is a place in Sussex, run by the Church, but that's mainly for women who go there to give birth. As for orphanages, Harold can get hold of some addresses for you, if it comes to that. I wonder if he might be persuaded to have a word with the girl's father? They have that great big old farmhouse. The young couple could quite well set up house in an unused room, and Matt could easily cycle to work from there.'

'And they'd be no worse off than many other young couples,' Maudie agreed. 'Very few young married people can afford to rent their own place right from the start, even if suitable accommodation was available. More often than not they spend the first few years in one parental home or the other. Mind you, it's not always a comfortable setting after the babies come, especially if they're living with his parents. I pity the bride who has to cope with a new baby and a mother-in-law at the same time!'

'I suppose you did your best with the

Blacks,' Mrs Blunt said. 'After all, you can only advise people. You cannot make decisions for them, or come between members of the family.'

'I can't help thinking that this will all end in tears,' Maudie said slowly.

'Well, that can't be avoided, can it? The poor girl can't marry the young man she loves — or thinks she loves, because she's so very young — and I wouldn't like to be in your shoes when the moment comes to steal her child away.'

'Thank you *very* much, Mrs Blunt.'

'I'm sorry, but isn't that what it amounts to?'

'Perhaps I'll be gone by then and the situation won't arise,' Maudie said.

'Has Dr Dean said anything more about your transfer, or whatever he wants to call it?'

'I haven't seen him again since he dropped his bombshell. As far as I know he's over at Midvale, trying to sort things out there. Hasn't Mr Blunt heard anything?'

'I know that he was going to sound out Councillor Reeves, who heads up the medical committee, but the man has been up in Newcastle for a few days, attending a family funeral. Have you thought about what you'd like to do if the worst comes to the worst?'

'I've thought about nothing else,' Maudie muttered. 'It might be nice to take a post in a posh nursing home, where the mothers would come to me rather my having to race through the rain on my bike to reach the patient. But those jobs are few and far between and I'm not sure if I'd like going back into a situation where I'd have to kowtow to a matron. What would I do if I signed on somewhere, only to find myself at the mercy of a female Hitler?'

'Throw a bedpan at her head I should imagine, knowing you as I do, Nurse Rouse!' They laughed at the thought.

★   ★   ★

'I suppose I could work as a district nurse,' Maudie mused. 'I do that sort of work half the time as it is. But I'd really hate to give up my midwifery. That's what

I'm trained for, and that's what I'd hoped to spend the rest of my working life doing. Who knows, maybe I was a midwife in a previous existence, if there's anything to Miss Blythe's fantasies. Perhaps I'm doomed to go through the centuries repeating my actions over and over again. It's a dismal thought.'

'Speaking of heartbreak,' Mrs Blunt said, 'what's the latest news on the Lily Willis front?'

'I haven't spoken to Mrs Willis recently but I'm sure we'd have heard something if there was anything to tell. The story is all round the district now, as you can imagine. Everyone is in sympathy with the family.'

The two women fell silent, lost in their own private thoughts. Lily, whose name wasn't Willis at all, had come to Llandyfan during the war as an evacuee, accompanied by her mother, Ruth Martin. The pair had been billeted on the Willises, who had a little girl of their own. Polly and Lily were much the same age and soon became fast friends.

Ruth had returned to London to visit

her ailing mother and had been killed in the blitz, or so everyone had thought. It wasn't until 1947 that it was revealed that the woman had survived the raids. She had later married an Australian serviceman and gone to live with him in his hometown. Now she wanted her daughter returned to her.

By this time Helen Willis thought of Lily as her own child, and certainly the two little girls were as close as any sisters could be. The thought of parting with the child was hard to swallow, but of far greater concern was how the change would affect Lily herself. The thought of what the child would have to endure distressed Maudie. How would the little girl feel if she were torn from everything and everybody she knew and loved, to travel thousands of miles away to live with a woman she barely remembered? If Maudie dreaded leaving Llandyfan, how much worse would it be for a child of eight? It didn't bear thinking about.

8

'Here, I've brought you some Mintoes,' Dick said, thrusting a small paper bag under Maudie's nose. 'Only two ounces, I'm afraid, but I know you like them.'

'Oh, Dick! You shouldn't spend your sweet ration on me.'

'Nonsense! I know they're your favourites. But if you feel guilty about it, you might let me have one or two for myself.'

Grinning, Maudie offered him the bag. 'What brought this on, anyway?'

'I was calling in on Mrs Hatch as it happens, and she was just replacing a jar of these on the shelf when I appeared.'

'Anything new on the shoplifting front?'

'No clue, I'm afraid, but it's still happening. Yesterday she found a tin of peaches missing, if you please! It's bad enough when everyday items talk a walk, but luxuries like peaches are so few and far between it doesn't seem fair that somebody will have to do without, simply because some unscrupulous person is at work.'

'Do you suppose it's a gang, gathering up merchandise to flog on the black market?'

Dick shook his head. 'I shouldn't think so. This is small potatoes in the scheme of things. It would hardly be worth their while. Besides, we haven't had any reports of problems elsewhere.'

Maudie unwrapped a sweet and put it in her mouth with a sigh of pleasure. 'What's on at the pictures this week, I wonder? I could do with a nice romantic story to take my mind off things.'

'*Brief Encounter* is on again,' Dick said, reaching for another sweet.

'I enjoyed that the first time around, but right now sitting through a weepie is the last thing I need.'

'I'm off on Saturday,' he said. 'If the weather keeps fine we could go off on our bikes and take a picnic with us. What do you say?'

'I'd love to go to the bluebell wood,' she told him. 'Why don't we . . . ' But whatever she meant to say was lost as the outer door banged and a breathless little boy almost fell at their feet.

'Mama says come!' he pleaded. 'You bring baby in bag, Nurse!'

The child's accent told them that he was not a local boy. In fact, Maude had never seen him before. She had a nodding acquaintance with most of the local children from her periodic visits to the school, and she was sure he wasn't a pupil there.

'Where do you live, dear?'

The little boy looked at her in bewilderment. 'Please?'

'Where is your mummy?'

'She stay at home.'

Patience, Maudie! Somewhere there is a woman depending on you, so don't frighten this little one away. 'Where is your home, dear?' she asked. The child continued to stare.

'Perhaps I can help,' Dick said. 'I'll take you in the car, and the youngster can point the way.'

The child now appeared to notice Dick for the first time, and he cowered against the wall, letting out a great wail. Maudie put a stop to this by popping her last remaining Mintoe into his mouth. His cries stopped abruptly.

'We'll load your bike in the back, Maudie,' Dick told her. 'If we're going any distance at all you'll probably need it to come back home on.'

By trial and error, with the little boy pointing a finger in the direction he thought they should take, the little party finally arrived at a disused railway siding. 'Looks like we've come to the wrong place,' Maudie muttered. 'The mother must have been desperate to send a child of that age for help. It's a miracle that he found us at all. Now what do we do next?'

But the child had slipped out of the car and was now racing towards a stand of trees, shouting for his mother as he went.

'He's heading for that abandoned railway carriage,' Dick said. 'Come on, old girl! I think we've found your expectant mother.'

Maudie snatched up her bag and followed. They entered the carriage by a door with the paint peeling off, and in the gloom she could just make out a woman, writhing on what had once been an upholstered seat for the use of passengers travelling by train.

Poor though the surroundings were, the interior of the carriage showed every sign of occupation. Pots and pans littered a makeshift table, on which a Primus stove held pride of place. Sagging blackout curtains covered some of the windows, while others were boarded up with the remains of packing crates. Brightly covered pictures, torn from magazines, were tacked to the wall. Someone had obviously gone to a great deal of trouble to make this place habitable.

Maudie approached the bed. 'Hello, I'm the midwife, Nurse Rouse. You sent your little boy to fetch me?' In a weak voice the woman spoke a few words in some language that was completely foreign to Maudie. She struggled to recall her schoolgirl French in case that might help, but the woman only shook her head by way of reply.

'This is a fine how'd-ye-do!' Maudie muttered, turning to Dick. 'You'll have to give me a hand here. Find out where they get their water and get that Primus going!'

'You want me to make tea?' he quipped, taking off his uniform jacket as he spoke.

'I want to examine my patient, so I'll ask you to wait outside, Dick Bryant. And you can take that little'un with you. He's scared enough as it is, poor little devil. Have a look around and see if there's a biscuit or a bit of bread and jam you can give him, to take his mind off what's happening here.'

'Right-ho!'

As she bent over her patient, Maudie reflected that Dick was a good man to have on hand in a crisis. Of course, that was only to be expected. He was a trained police officer. She had never considered the fact before, but she wondered now if he'd had any training in delivering a baby in an emergency. You occasionally heard of policemen or taxi drivers bringing babies into the world, but were they competent at the job? Or did they just stand there, frightened to death, waiting to take a slippery, blood-covered newborn into their hands? When all this was over she would have to ask him.

There were no cupboards, but Dick came across a series of orange boxes that apparently did duty as a place to store food. Having looked through two of them without finding biscuits he turned to the third, and his mouth dropped open when he saw what it contained. There were three tins of Fray Bentos corned beef, six tins of Spam and one lonely can of peaches. Apparently he had discovered the grocery shop thief.

The little boy pointed to the peaches in delight. 'Me five!' he chuckled.

Dick took that to mean that the child was about to have a birthday, with the fruit meant as a special treat. A small, flat package wrapped in newspaper was concealed behind the tins. 'No prizes for guessing what his birthday present is,' Dick thought with a pang. If that did not contain a bar of Fry's peppermint cream, he was a monkey's uncle.

'Is that water boiling yet?' Maudie called.

'Ready in two ticks,' he responded.

There were times when he hated his job. Of course he would have to turn this woman in; you couldn't let a thief go free. On the other hand, these people had so little. It seemed the worst cruelty to inflict more punishment on them.

By the look of things these were displaced persons, or DPs as the population of England knew them. Thousands of people who had lost everything when their homelands had been overtaken by war now had to rebuild their shattered live as best they could. England, too, had its share of people who had lost their homes during the heavy bombing of its major cities, and many of them were reduced to living in abandoned Nissen huts, or train carriages like this one.

The authorities were doing their best to re-home people. Modest prefabricated housing had been built in some towns, and councils everywhere were struggling to erect affordable housing for its citizens, but it was a slow process.

A high-pitched scream from the woman on the bed, followed by Maudie's low tones of reassurance, interrupted Dick's train of thought. Grabbing a galvanized pail, he went in search of more water.

9

'I've come for the Box, please,' Maudie told Mrs Blunt the following morning. This was a collection of first-size baby garments, available to go out on loan to needy mothers of the parish who would eventually launder them and return them to the church. The scheme had been started in the days when Queen Victoria ruled the empire, and wages for agricultural labourers were low. Many people were living hand-to-mouth, and with the best will in the world they could not afford to dress the children in their enormous families.

The custom had fallen by the wayside during the prosperous days of the Edwardian era, but the experiences of two world wars had brought renewed hardship to country places. Women trying to manage on a meagre army pension while their husbands were serving abroad were thankful to have access to baby clothes, however faded and worn. Any clothing that came into the shops was strictly rationed, so everyone was in the same boat when it came to looking shabby.

'Oh, that's all taken care of, Nurse,' Mrs Blunt said cheerfully. My husband called in to see the poor woman last night and he delivered the box at the same time. You're just off to see her now, I take it?'

'That's right.'

'What did she have, Nurse? A boy or a girl? I asked Harold but he didn't have a clue. Said he didn't like to ask. Can you believe it?'

Maudie laughed. 'A lovely little girl. Don't ask me what she weighed. Her mother is too poor to own kitchen scales, so we'll have to wait until she brings the baby in for a check-up. Look here, Mrs Blunt, I know we can't do much about their living conditions, but there's a lot we can do to make the place more comfortable for them. Do you suppose we could get the locals to have a whip-round in the Royal Oak, or something?'

Now it was Mrs Blunt's turn to

chuckle. 'Fear not, Nurse. The Women's Institute has everything in hand. Blankets and food supplies are already on their way, and someone has dusted off an old cot so that poor baby won't have to spend its first weeks in that old cardboard box you found.'

'And a jolly good thing, too. You know, Mrs Blunt, I've been known to tuck up a new baby into a dresser drawer when no cot was available, but these people don't even possess a chest of drawers. Now, what I want to know is, where is this woman's husband? And why is she out there trying to manage all alone?'

The vicar's wife looked smug. 'Well, now, I can fill you in on that. He's gone to Cardiff, trying to get work on the docks. If he succeeds he'll send for his family, but in the meantime he left Mrs Yolkowskie here because she was too close to her time, and not fit to travel.'

Maudie's mouth dropped open. 'How on earth . . . ?'

'Harold got hold of a Polish chap who works on a farm out on the road to Midvale. On the off-chance that the woman might speak the language he took him along, and sure enough, she is Polish too.'

'Well, I never,' Maudie said. 'Yolkowskie?' she asked, rolling the name around in an attempt to get the pronunciation straight.

'Yes. The little boy is Ambrose, and the baby is to be called Barbara.'

'I'm glad the community is rallying round, but there's still something to worry about. It turns out that this woman is the shoplifter Mrs Hatch has had such trouble with. I hate to think what may happen when the case come up before the magistrates. What becomes of the children if their mother gets sent down? A new baby needs its mother.'

'Actually, that's all taken care of as well. Mrs Yolkowskie confessed everything to Harold. Oh, I don't mean confession in that sense — he is Church of England after all, although these Polish people are Catholics and perhaps she thinks he has special powers. Apparently she hasn't received any money from her husband for several weeks, and of course if he hasn't found work then he won't have had anything to send. Anyway, she's been going into the shop, buying a few odds and ends with what little cash she has, and slipping a few extras into her apron pocket when Mrs Hatch is otherwise occupied. Mrs Hatch hasn't noticed anything amiss because of the language barrier, you see. She hardly speaks to the woman other than to tot up her purchases, and the poor soul holds out the money, which is completely foreign to her, having to trust Mrs Hatch to hand over the correct change.'

'Oh, dear.'

'Anyway, after hearing what Harold had to say, Mrs Hatch has decided not to press charges, and neither will she ask to have the stolen goods returned.'

'That's good of her, I must say.'

Mrs Blunt smiled slyly. 'She's a good Christian woman, and a pillar of the Mothers' Union. Besides, she won't lose by it. She's put up a notice in the shop asking people to donate groceries to the family. Of course, they'll buy them in her shop, so there will be a bit of profit in it for her.'

'Naturally.'

'And I thought we could give a birthday party for the little boy, here in the parish hall. We'll invite a few kiddies of his age and I'll see if I can manage a birthday cake. He deserves a treat after managing so bravely to fetch help for his mother.'

Maudie cycled off, her faith in human nature renewed.

★   ★   ★

She found Mrs Yolkowskie sitting up in bed, feeding her infant. Little Ambrose was sitting on the floor, pushing a block of wood around, making *vroom-vroom* noises. Maudie made a mental note to buy him a little toy car for his birthday, if she could find one in the shops. Dinky Cars were good value, and it might be the start of a collection for him.

Recognizing Maudie, the woman smiled. Now came the problem of communicating with smiles and gestures. 'Barbara!' Maudie said, caressing the baby's small downy head.

'Helena!' Mrs Yolkowskie pointed to herself.

'Nurse Rouse,' Maudie responded. 'Your husband?' she mouthed, pointing to the ring on Helena's hand, and then to her own bare fingers.

Helena reached under her pillow — at least she possessed that! — and brought out a small handbag. She extracted a bent studio portrait, which she handed to Maudie.

The photograph showed a young couple with a baby. The dark-haired husband was neatly dressed in a suit and tie, while the woman wore a pretty summer frock, with a smart hat perched on the side of her head. Their baby was dressed in long white garments trimmed with lace, and Maudie guessed that the photo had been taken to commemorate his baptism.

'Josef,' Mrs Yolkowskie explained, jabbing a finger at the man in the picture. 'Ambrose!' That, of course, was the child who was with them now. Finally she pointed to the woman in the photo and then to herself. The person portrayed there bore no resemblance to the woman on the bed, whose hair was lank and her skin blotched. This was what war did to people. Just a few short years ago this prosperous-looking couple had lived a life full of hope, proud of their first son and expecting to see him grow up into a successful man.

Just look at them now! Tears sprang to Maudie's eyes, quickly suppressed. One of the first things she'd been taught as a nurse was not to get emotionally involved with the patients. But how could you remain human if you didn't care? She counseled herself to look on the bright side. The Yolkowskies had survived the war. They were alive. They were blessed with two beautiful, healthy children. God willing, they would find their way in what was to them an alien land, and young Barbara would never know what war meant.

Her examination of mother and baby over, Maudie joined the woman in a cup of tea. She rather hoped that the family would stay in the area. Ambrose would be eligible to start school in the autumn, and after that his language skills would improve by leaps and bounds. In turn, he would be able to teach his mother the English she would need to help her fit into her new surroundings.

'Try to stay in bed and get some rest,' she advised, uncomfortably aware that Helena probably had no idea as to what she was trying to convey. She patted the bed then pointed at the young mother. 'You stay!' Helena smiled and shrugged. 'Never mind,' Maudie told her. 'I'll come back this evening and bring you some soup.'

'Soup!' Ambrose said, smacking his lips.

'Yes, yes, you shall have some too,' Maudie said, although whether he understood what she was saying, or simply mimicking the sound of her voice, she had no way of telling.

10

Maudie called at the Blacks' home to see how Greta was doing. She was thankful to learn that Frank was away from home, having gone to see about a spare part for his tractor, according to his wife. She could do without another lecture on her duties to this household with him demanding to know how she was getting on with finding an adoptive home for the coming baby.

'She's in the sitting room with those film magazines of hers,' Mrs Black grunted. 'She won't do a hand's turn, that girl. You could darn your dad's socks, I told her, but will she? Not on your life. She won't even shell a basin of peas for me. Kids! I don't know; you give birth to them in agony, honestly determined to bring them up to be a credit to you, and then after all that they let you down. That girl needs to buck her ideas up, or who knows what's to become of her?'

'She is eight and a half months gone, Mrs Black,' Maudie said mildly. 'At this stage she won't feel like moving too fast, although she really should be taking some gentle exercise. I'll see if I can persuade her to get outside in the sunshine for half an hour.'

Maudie was not looking forward to her meeting with Greta. Thanks to her father's ultimatum, the girl had been forbidden to see her boyfriend and she was about to lose her child as well. The girl was bound to be in great distress. Of course, it might be best if the baby did go to a good home, leaving her free to pick up the pieces of her life, but would she be grateful for that reprieve, or simply devastated? Swallowing hard, Maudie knocked on the sitting room door and marched in without waiting for an answer.

Greta, with her feet up on the sofa, was idly turning the pages of a film magazine. Far from being depressed, she seemed almost joyful. She looked up when Maudie entered, turning the publication around to display the article she was engrossed in. 'See this, Nurse? It's all about Elizabeth Taylor.'

'Oh, yes?'

'She's ever so lovely. This here calls her 'enchantingly beautiful'.'

'Fancy!'

'It says she has violet eyes. Do you think that's true? I mean, that's purple, isn't it? I don't know anybody that has purple eyes.'

'I'm sure that's an exaggeration,' Maudie said. 'Now then, I want to examine you, if I may.'

Greta looked at her dreamily. 'She's two years younger than me, Nurse, and she's a famous star already. Did you see *National Velvet*? Oh, I loved that! I sat through it three times, and if it ever comes round again I'll have to go back. I do hope she makes more pictures. Do you think she will, Nurse?'

'I doubt it,' Maudie remarked, glance at the publicity shot of the fifteen-year-old acting sensation. 'These child stars are all the same. They shine brightly for a while and then they sink without trace. We shan't be hearing much more of Miss Elizabeth Taylor, you can count on that.'

'Aw, Nurse! Don't be such a spoil-sport!' Greta took a last, loving look at her idol before tossing the magazine side. Maudie lifted the girl's maternity smock and began her examination. She noted that the baby's position had changed slightly, which indicated that labour would begin within a couple of weeks. 'You haven't felt any pains, have you, Greta?' she asked.

The girl's eyes widened in alarm. 'Pains? What's the matter with me, Nurse? Has something gone wrong with the baby?'

Maudie hastened to reassure her. 'No, no. Everything is as it should be. It's just that women sometimes experience what we call false labour, contractions that prepare your muscles for delivery. Not everyone gets them, and when they do, the pains come and go.'

'If I get them will it hurt?'

'At that stage the pains are quite mild, and you may not get them anyway. But I do advise you to take some gentle exercise, Greta. You should have been out for a walk every day. Keeping yourself limbered up will help you when your time comes.'

Greta scowled. 'You sound like Mum. Always keeping on at me, she is. Telling me I'll be sorry if I don't get up and do things when all I really want is to lie down! What does she know about it, anyway?'

Quite a lot, I imagine, Maudie thought. Mrs Black had given birth to Greta seventeen years earlier and had experienced two miscarriages since. The prospective grandmother was an old hand at the birthing game. Maudie grinned as another thought occurred to her. She herself was the expert here on matters of maternity, yet she had not given birth personally. In some ways she was no more experienced than the girl beside her, never having felt the pangs associated with pushing a baby into the world.

'What is it, Nurse? What's funny?'

'Oh, nothing. Now you just remember what I said, Greta, and go out for a little walk. It's for your own good, you know. Otherwise everything is progressing normally, and all things considered I'm glad to find you looking so cheerful.'

'How do you mean?'

'Well, I know you love young Matt, but hasn't your father forbidden you to see him?'

A curious expression flitted across Greta's face. 'Oh, Dad! I don't pay no attention to him. He's in for a surprise, he is!'

'A surprise? What sort of surprise?'

But Greta only picked up her magazine and began to turn the pages. It was quite clear that she was determined to say no more. Frustrated, Maudie repacked her black bag and left the room.

Panting slightly as she cycled against the wind, Maudie wondered what the girl could have meant. Greta and her mother must have discussed their dilemma; was it possible that they intended to defy Frank Black and insist on keeping the baby? If they did, he wasn't the only one who was in for a surprise. Once the baby was here, disrupting the household with its demands and keeping everyone awake at night, his determination to rid them of the child would reach new heights. What would he do then? Leave the baby on the church steps? Deliver it to an orphanage, thrusting it into the arms of a startled matron?

She slowed down when she saw an elderly woman perched on a stile at the side of the road. It was Miss Blythe, of all people. Just what she didn't need on a busy morning!

'Good morning, Miss Blythe. Are you all right? Not feeling faint, are you?'

'Oh, it's you, Nurse. No, I've just stopped for a little rest, that's all.'

'Are you sure you're all right? You're a long way from the Royal Oak; it must be two miles at least.'

'That's always been my trouble, Nurse. I set out handily enough and walk until I'm tired, quite forgetting that I have to cover the same distance on the way back. Never mind. I'll just sit here till I recover my puff and then I'll be off again. I'll just put one foot in front of the other and keep moving. That's the way to do it!'

'I wish that some of my patients thought as you do, Miss Blythe. I'm glad to see that you've recovered from your nasty accident at the river.'

'Accident, is it? So you're like the rest of them, are you? I've explained that I was pushed! There was a deliberate attempt to silence me, Nurse!'

Maudie knew she should leave well alone and push on to see her next patient, but she loved a mystery and she longed to get to the bottom of this one. What would Miss Marple do? Maudie was a great fan of Agatha Christie's books, and of all the author's characters she liked the elderly sleuth the best. After all, she herself was another village spinster, although not yet of a certain age.

'Who would want to kill you, Miss Blythe?' she asked getting off her bicycle and leaning it against the fence.

'Ah, now that would be telling!'

'Can't you at least tell me why anyone should want you dead? For instance, who would profit by your death?'

'I have no wealth to leave!'

'Oh? But you must have some assets,

surely? How else can you pay your way at the Royal Oak?'

Miss Blythe leapt to her feet with surprisingly agility for one of her age. 'You are the most impertinent woman, Nurse!' she snapped, as she heaved herself over the stile. Maudie stood still in stupefaction as the women stumped her way across a field, heading goodness knew where.

11

Maudie had invited Dick Bryant to come to her cottage for his tea. This was taking their relationship to a new level, but two of her expectant mothers were nearing their time and she didn't want to go far from the village. He had invited her to go to the pictures in Midvale and she was afraid he'd be hurt if she kept turning down his invitations.

This seemed like a good alternative. They could enjoy a good meal and then settle in to listen to Paul Temple on the wireless before Dick had to catch the last bus home. Both of them hated to miss an episode of the BBC serial featuring the mystery-solving amateur detective.

Meanwhile, Maudie had to solve a mystery of a purely domestic kind: what to feed her man. She'd asked him what he fancied to eat and he'd been no help at all.

'Anything you'd like to serve up,' he

told her. 'Beans on toast?'

'But what is your favourite food?'

'Deep-fried pork pie. Scrumptious!'

Maudie thought longingly of a Melton Mowbray pie with its thick pastry, spicy filling and bits of savoury jelly. No doubt it would be delicious when heated in sizzling fat, but she didn't possess a deep enough pot in which to prepare it. Perhaps she could get hold of some lamb cutlets to serve with peas, golden roast potatoes and mint sauce. Or would cauliflower cheese be sufficient? Something she could prepare ahead of time and heat up at the last moment, if one or both of them should be delayed? She could see that problems like this must be an irritant to the average housewife, especially with food rationing still in force. Oh for the glorious day to come when you could just go out and take your pick from shops brimming with food! Would that day ever come?

Serving a full meal would involve her taking the bus into town, where she would have to stand in line at the butcher's shop or the fishmonger's. Mrs

Hatch's little shop was convenient for Maudie's needs most of the time, but her stock was limited. She finally settled on a corned beef pie made in a casserole dish. She had a light hand with pastry; and a filling of the tinned meat, mixed with onions and Bisto gravy, should be tasty enough to satisfy any man. Any leftovers could be eaten cold the following day.

What could she give him for afters? She'd heard him say he was partial to apple tart and custard, but it wouldn't do to serve two lots of pastry in the same meal. Looking around for inspiration, she found half a tin of cocoa at the back of her store cupboard; she might make a chocolate blancmange.

She made a list of things to do on the day. She would lay a fire so that all she had to do was set a match to it when the time came. She would lay the table with her favourite willow pattern plates and the cork mats with pictures of Westminster Abbey on them. A vase of flowers would provide a nice finishing touch — or would that be over the top? Heaven forbid the table should look like the setting for a marriage proposal! She would be so embarrassed if Dick got the idea that she was trying to trap him!

★   ★   ★

Meanwhile, there were other social engagements to prepare for. 'We've found out when the little boy's birthday is,' Mrs Blunt told her. 'Thank goodness Harold found that Polish chap to translate for us, or we'd never be able to communicate with Mrs Yolkowskie. I've invited the whole infants' class from the Sunday School and naturally enough everyone is delighted. All kiddies love a party.'

'And it's killing two birds with one stone,' Maudie remarked, 'because all those children will be starting school together in the autumn. What are we going to do about food for the party?'

'Oh, that's all sorted. Each of the mothers will bring one thing: jelly or sandwiches or fairy cakes. I've promised to contribute the birthday cake, I only hope I can get hold of some candles to put on it. It's been many a long day since candles were used on a birthday cake in this house.'

'What about games?'

'Ah, now that's where you come in, Nurse.'

'Me?'

'We'll be having games, of course: musical chairs and pin the tail on the donkey — the usual things — and I wondered if you could rustle up some little prizes. Nothing too expensive, mind you; perhaps crayons or a few sweeties.'

'Just as long as they don't expect me to hand out babies from my black bag!' Maudie joked. 'I take it you won't be going the whole hog, then, putting on a Punch and Judy show, or hiring a conjuror?'

'I'm afraid we can't run to anything like that, but five-year-olds are easily satisfied. We'll keep more interesting entertainments in mind for the church fête.'

'Such as?'

'Oh, the usual things. Sack races and the tug-of-war for the men, egg and spoon races for the youngsters, tables selling jams and jellies and knitted bed socks.'

94

'And Gypsy Rose Lee telling fortunes for the benefit of silly young girls?'

'Really, Nurse! Gypsy Rose Lee is an American striptease artiste! Even *I* know that. Llandyfan would never recover from the shock! Mind you, Harold is in two minds whether to allow a fortune teller's tent at all this year.'

'It's pretty harmless, though. You cross the gypsy's palm with silver and in return she tells you about a tall dark stranger and mysterious journeys abroad. Everybody goes away happy and the church roof fund is a few bob richer. Money for jam!'

A worried look crossed Mrs Blunt's face. 'I admit that's usually the case, but this year it may be different.'

'How so?'

'You know Miss Blythe, of course.'

'Don't tell me she's prepared to put her hair up in a turban and sit in a darkened tent, dispensing the wisdom of the ages?'

'If only it were that simple. No, her sister is returning from America and apparently she's a sort of psychic who does readings for people who want to see into the future. Madam Zora, she calls herself. Miss Blythe tells me that her sister will perform for us free of charge if Harold will agree to it.'

'So then we'll have Miss Blythe, with her experience of her past lives, and now her sister, who can project herself into the future. What a family! I do believe that having Madam Zora at the fête will be a smashing success. The whole village knows about Miss Blythe and her ten children and they'll be bursting to see what her sister has to tell them. You can't lose!'

'That's just the trouble. This is the Church of England, Nurse, and this fortunetelling business smacks of the occult. Harold is quite uneasy about it, and I can't think what the bishop will say. If we allow this sort of thing, what comes next? Séances in the vestry? Halloween gatherings in the graveyard?'

'Oh, I'm sure people will have much more mundane concerns,' Maudie said. 'You know the sort of thing. Will I win the football pools? When will rationing end?

When will my boyfriend pop the question? As a matter of fact I'd like a few questions answered myself!'

'Aha! Are you hoping that the handsome constable will have something to propose when he comes to your cottage for his tea?' Mrs Blunt asked, with a knowing smile.' You are such a sly boots, Nurse. You know what they say about the way to a man's heart being through his stomach.'

'No such thing,' Maudie told her, blushing. 'As a matter of fact, I thought I'd better try to do some entertaining in my cottage while I still have it. I've always meant to do more of that sort of thing — perhaps invite a few women in for whist and a cup of tea, or something, but somehow I've never got round to it. It's never wise to plan too far ahead in my job, you know. Babies are apt to put in an appearance at the most inconvenient times.'

'You haven't heard any more about your job, then.'

'It's not just that. Dr Dean dropped in again yesterday for a word with me about his accommodation. The cheek of the man! He seems to think I should just stand aside and vacate my home and let him move in. Can I be made to move, Mrs Blunt? I've always paid my rent on time and been a good tenant. The trouble is, the place goes with the job, so it's a tied cottage in a way. It's owned by the council, and so am I, in a manner of speaking. I'm afraid they might think it more important to house the new doctor, but I've lived alone for a long time and I don't want to go back to living in digs. My student days are long over.'

'Where is Dr Dean staying at the moment?'

'At Dr Mallory's. The problem is, there's no privacy there. The surgery is right there in the house, with patients crowding in on a daily basis. Miss Holmes is there on the spot five days a week. Dr Mallory and his ancient housekeeper live on the premises and Dr Dean has been pitchforked into the middle of all that. I can quite see that he must long to find a place of his own, where he can unwind after working hours, or entertain friends.

He's entitled to that, after all his years of training as a doctor, but why does it have to be at my expense?'

'Don't worry, Nurse,' Mrs Blunt told her. 'If the worst comes to the worst, there will always be a home for you here.'

Her friend's kindness brought tears to Maudie's eyes. She stood up suddenly, saying that she had to go. It was only when she was fitting the key into her front door that she thought about the way in which the vicar's wife had made her generous offer. Did she know something she couldn't tell Maudie? Otherwise, wouldn't she have assured her that she was quite safe from eviction, for it would never come to that? As for the council letting her know where she stood, rot their socks! And as for Dr Dean, just who did he think he was?

12

Maudie laughed when Dick came into the house sniffing like a Bisto kid in the advertisements.

'Are you hungry?' she asked. 'It won't be long.'

'I've starved myself all day getting ready for this. I've decided that was the best way, in case you can't cook! If I'm hungry enough I can eat anything.'

'Cheek!'

'By the smell of it, though, you've got something really tasty on the go.'

He certainly did justice to her corned beef pie, and any thoughts she might have had about holding back leftovers for her lunch the next day quickly disappeared. She had served it with plenty of creamed mashed potato, diced carrots and thinly sliced runner beans.

His eyes brightened when he saw the blancmange. 'Chocolate shape! My old gran used to make that for me as a treat when I spent my holidays with her as child. She made it in a fancy mould so the blancmange had knobs on top when she turned it out onto a plate.'

'No knobs here, I'm afraid,' Maudie said. 'There's top of the milk, though, if you fancy that. Is your grandmother still alive?'

'No. Sadly, she died in 1932. Just as well, really. Two of my uncles were killed in the war, one fighting at Dieppe and the other in North Africa. At least she was spared that, poor old girl. I always think it's so sad when parents outlive their children.'

'I know,' Maudie agreed, but she was thinking of some of the grief she'd witnessed during her nursing career — people who had lost their children to scarlet fever or meningitis, or whose babies were stillborn. But there were to be no gloomy thoughts tonight.

'I'm going to leave these things in the sink to soak and then we'll move over to the fire,' she murmured. Her little cottage did not boast a dining room, and since this was a special occasion she hadn't wanted to serve the meal in the kitchen. They were eating at her prized drop-leaf table in the sitting room. 'I'll bring in some hot drinks in a minute. What will you have? Tea, Camp coffee, or Ovaltine? And if you're still hungry I have cheese and biscuits. Cream crackers, that is, with a piece of rat trap!'

'You've done me proud, Maudie. I couldn't eat another thing. A strong cup of tea would go down a treat, though.'

Maudie was delighted with the success of her simple meal. Now they would sit in companionable silence, listening to the exploits of Paul Temple. The amateur sleuth was an author who solved crimes with the help of his journalist wife, who was known as Steve because her pen name was Steve Trent. 'Just like us!' Maudie whispered as she waited for the kettle to boil. Not that she would ever have shared that thought with Dick. He was a police officer, a professional, while she was . . . what? Just a would-be Miss Marple. But she had helped Dick in the past; he could not deny that. After discovering the corpse of the murdered man, Cyril Swain, she had doggedly followed up every clue that presented itself. Of course the police had done their bit, but without her input they might never have caught up with the killer, who had been poised to emigrate to Australia.

'Hurry up, Maudie! It's about to start,' Dick called from the other room. The thrilling tones of the programme's new signature tune, *Coronation Scot*, came to her ears.

'Just coming!' Her fantasy continued. When the programme ended they would continue to sit beside the fire, chatting, until it was time for Dick to go for his bus. Then, standing on the doorstep, surely they might exchange a kiss. It might be just a peck on the cheek, as between friends — or, might it amount to something more?

'Come *on!*' Dick bellowed. 'You'll miss the start!'

★ ★ ★

Maudie stretched out her legs towards the fire. She felt that she was looking her best. She wore her best crimson jumper, with a navy blue skirt that was only slightly out of date. Carefully hoarded silk stockings completed the ensemble. She'd had them since before the war and they were almost as good as new, except for one tiny darn in a place where it wouldn't show.

Maudie didn't have much in the way of mufti and that wasn't just because of wartime restrictions. For most of her life she had worn uniform of one sort or another, either at school, or in the Guides, or as a nurse. Apart from that, all she really needed was one set of best clothes for going to church on Sunday.

Dick was used to seeing her in her nurse's uniform, garments that were practical rather than attractive. Had he noticed the difference now? He hadn't said anything. He'd reserved his compliments for her cookery, which had received rave reviews. At her age, perhaps that was the best she could hope for? Considering this, she laughed out loud.

Dick looked up in surprise. 'What's the matter with you, old girl? Paul is unarmed, feeling his way into the house in the dark, not realizing that the villain is waiting behind the door with his cosh raised to strike!'

'Oh, is he? Sorry about that! I was thinking of something else.'

Dick grunted. Lesson number two, Maudie reminded herself: never come between your man and his obsessions. That was the worst part of living alone, she supposed; you became used to talking to yourself, or to the cat, or breaking into insane laughter when something tickled your funny bone. Interacting socially with other people meant holding yourself in check at all times.

She had lost the thread of the story now. By the sound of things, Paul was engaged in an all-out fracas with unseen villains. Would Steve turn up in time to frighten off the intruder, or would she, too, be in danger of a bashing?

Outside the cottage a stiff wind had blown up, and rain came pelting down in sheets. Seemingly they were in for a stormy night, and Dick would get soaked while he waited for his bus. Thinking of that, Maudie was thoroughly distracted now.

For two pins she would have turned off the wireless, but that wouldn't be fair to Dick, who was still engrossed in the plot. She was suddenly aware of a droning noise in the background that had nothing to do with Paul Temple. It sounded like a motorcycle, and one that was coming closer by the minute. The sound stopped abruptly and then she almost jumped out of her skin as a volley of heavy raps assaulted the front door.

'Who on earth can that be at this time of night?' she said, jumping to her feet. In Maudie's life, dramatic interruptions usually mean the imminent arrival of a baby. There was no question of refusing to answer the door.

'You'd better let me go,' Dick said. 'It could be someone who has had one too many at the Royal Oak.'

In the end they got there at the same time. Maudie was forced to flatten herself against the wall of the tiny hall as Dick flung the door open.

The man on the doorstep had light

brown hair, plastered to his skull by the rain. 'Accident at the crossroads!' he gasped, looking at Maudie with frightened brown eyes. 'Some people are hurt, and I've heard you're a nurse. Can you come? I can give you a lift if you don't mind riding pillion.'

Maudie reached for her Burberry, which was on its usual hook near the door. 'Just hang on while I fetch my bag,' she ordered,' cramming her hat down on her head as she flew back to the living room.

'And has anyone called for an ambulance?' Dick asked. 'No? Then I'll do that now. And where's your bike, Maudie? I'll borrow that and follow on behind you.'

'In the coal shed,' she told him, thrusting a pile of towels into an oilcloth bag as she spoke. 'And don't forget to lock up when you leave.' She thrust her bags into one of the motorcycle's panniers, which fortunately was empty.

They drove off into the night, with Maudie holding her hat down with one hand while clinging to the belt of the young man's mac with the other.

* ★ *

The scene that met Maudie's eyes as the motorcycle skidded to a halt looked like an illustration from the *Boy's Own Paper*. Her legs felt like rubber as she dismounted from the powerful machine, but she managed to walk towards the carnage without displaying any fear or hesitation.

What looked like a very elderly Austin 7 was lying across the narrow road, with its nose in the ditch. Another car, with its headlights blazing, had stopped some distance away. An elderly man hurried forward, greeting Maudie with relief.

13

'Are you the nurse?' The man looked as if he was about to be sick.

'That's right. Are you hurt any way?'

'What? Oh, no. I wasn't in the accident. I came along just after it happened, as did your young escort there. I thought I'd better stay here and keep my lights on to warn people, or there could be more been trouble if someone else comes pelting round that blind corner.'

'Quick thinking,' Maudie said. 'A policeman will be along in a minute and he'll tell you what to do next. In the meantime I'd better have a look inside that car, or what's left of it.'

The silence was ominous. At the very least the occupants must be unconscious. If anyone was still alive in the wreckage, Maudie prayed that they wouldn't be suffering from head or spinal injuries.

Suddenly, however, the silence was broken by a piercing scream. Maudie tensed. She knew that tone only too well. That sound was not coming from a man with something like a broken leg. It was the cry of a woman caught in the throes of bringing new life into the world. She broke into a trot, only pausing to call back over her shoulder to the two men who stood dithering at the roadside.

'Move that car so the light shines on the wreckage!' she bawled. 'If I have to deliver a baby here I don't want to do it in the dark!'

The back door of the crumpled Austin was broken off and Maudie peered inside, following the sound of the groans made by the labouring woman.

'Is that you, Nurse? Oh, thank goodness! I thought I was going to die here all alone.'

Maudie frowned. 'That's not you, is it, Greta? What on earth are you doing out here like this? No, never mind. Explanations can wait. I'll just have a quick look at you, and then we'll sit tight and wait for the ambulance to come. It should be along soon.'

Greta was stretched out on the back

seat, which had probably saved her life, for had she been sitting in the passenger seat she could have been crushed by the impact. There was no movement from whoever was in the driver's seat.

'Fully dilated!' Maudie told herself when she had carried out her examination in the gloom. Unless a miracle occurred, the baby would be well on its way before that ambulance arrived. There was no point in trying to maintain her undignified crouch over the girl's legs. It wouldn't do to wobble when she needed both hands to receive the slippery baby.

With a sigh of resignation she went down on her knees on the wet gravel, bidding a rueful goodbye to her good stockings. Caught in the headlights of the other car, she was not about to treat the watching men to a display of suspender belt and knickered leg by removing the stockings in public!

'Where's Matt? Is Matt all right?' Greta cried, struggling to sit up. 'He's not dead, is he?'

'Of course not,' Maudie lied. In a very short time the girl would need all her strength to push her baby into the world; there was no future in letting her fret over the probable death of the child's father. Fortunately there was no time for further conversation, as Greta let out a shriek of pain and distress. The second stage of labour had begun.

'Remember how I showed you how to pant?' Maudie said. 'Good girl! That's right.'

'I'm going to die, aren't I? Matt's dead and I'm going to die too!'

'Nonsense! Of course you're not going to die. I shan't let you.'

'Where's that ambulance, then? You said the ambulance was coming. Why isn't it here?'

'Just what I'd like to know,' Maudie muttered under her breath. 'We don't really need it,' she told the panicking girl. 'If you were having this baby at home — as you should have been — we certainly wouldn't call one. I'm in charge, my girl, and everything is going to be all right.'

'Constable Dick Bryan, reporting for duty,' said a voice in Maudie's ear. She looked up with a smile. 'Right, then. You can just hold that torch a little closer if you don't mind, so I can see what I'm up to.'

'What's he doing here?' Greta gasped. 'Tell him to go away! I don't want him seeing me like this!'

'This is no time to come over all modest,' Maudie told her. 'You don't want me to drop the baby, do you? As for you, Dick, open that bag for me, will you? No, not that one. The oilcloth bag with the towels in it. I'll need something to wrap the baby in when it gets here. I don't suppose you brought any baby clothes with you, Greta?'

'I haven't got any, Nurse.'

'And why not, pray?'

'It was Dad. He wouldn't let us buy anything, because he said you'd be taking the baby away with you as soon as it was born. I wouldn't even be allowed to see it. Mum did start knitting a little matinee coat, but when he saw what she was doing he ripped the stitches off the needles and she didn't dare start up again.'

This unlovely tale was interrupted by

another shriek of agony. 'It won't be long now, dear,' Maudie assured the frightened teenager.

Baby Boy Black came squalling into the world just as the ambulance came round the curve in the road, apparently travelling with only three wheels on the tarmac. Dick patted Maudie on the shoulder. 'Well done, by Timothy!' he said, quoting Paul Temple.

'It's not over yet,' Maudie told him. 'The afterbirth is still to come, but in the meantime you can hold this little chap while I cut the cord.'

'You took your time!' she grunted when the first of the ambulance attendants joined them, carrying powerful lanterns.

'Sorry and all that! This isn't the only accident we've had to deal with tonight. Are you hurt, missus? That looks like blood on your hands!'

'I'm the local midwife, Nurse Rouse to you,' Maudie informed him. 'And I've a mother and newborn baby here. And no,' she continued, as it appeared that the man was about to crawl into the back of the car, 'you can't move them yet. But if you have a basin or a bucket handy I'll need something to put the placenta in.'

'And I'm Constable Bryant,' Dick said, asserting his authority in case they thought he was just a nosy bystander because he wasn't in uniform. 'There's a chap in the driver's seat but I haven't been able to rouse him. Better see to him first.'

Her job completed, Maudie stood by, holding the mewling infant while the men loaded Greta into the ambulance. She was glad to see that when the stretcher holding Matt was placed in the waiting vehicle, his face wasn't covered by the red blanket. That must mean he was still alive, although for how long that state of affairs would continue obviously depended on the state of his injuries.

'I'm coming too,' Maudie announced. She feared that because of the poor visibility, her examination of the afterbirth had been cursory at best. It was vitally important to check that it had come away completely, otherwise a post-partum haemorrhage could occur. Then, too, she wanted to stay with Greta and her baby until they were safely handed over to the staff at the cottage hospital.

'I'm staying here,' Dick told her. 'There will be a police car here any time now, and meanwhile I want to interview those two chaps to see what they can tell us about the accident. Then they can go on their way.'

'They won't be able to tell you much,' Maudie answered. 'The driver of the other car said the smash had already happened by the time he arrived on the scene, and he stayed on to warn others who might come upon it and be unable to stop.'

*　*　*

'You look like you've been in the wars,' the night sister remarked when Maudie had been relieved of her charges at the cottage hospital and made her report. 'Why don't you go and have a wash and brush up, and then I'll see about getting you a cup of tea and a sandwich.'

'I could certainly do with one,' Maudie sighed, 'and so, I'm sure, could young

Greta. After asking if the baby is all right, with all its fingers and toes, that's the first thing my mothers ask for — a good strong cup of tea!'

By the time she had tidied herself up and seen Greta safely installed in her hospital bed, Maudie was almost asleep on her feet. She was glad when the night sister led the way to her private domain, a tiny room furnished with a desk and two armchairs.

'Do sit down, Nurse. Thanks to the stormy weather, it's been a busy night with several admissions, but now it's 'All quiet on the Western Front'. Do you take sugar?'

Sister Tranter hadn't met Maudie before and she was eager to hear about the midwife's experiences in the Llandy-fan district.

'I love it there,' Maudie admitted, 'but I'm afraid I may not be there much longer.'

'Why on earth not?'

'None of us quite know what to expect from this new National Health scheme. On the face of it, life should be easier all round for patients and nurses alike, but there are sure to be problems to iron out at first. On top of that, we've been landed with a very officious new doctor, a certain Dr Dean.'

The sister made a wry face. 'Dr Donald Dean? Oh, him!'

14

Home at last! After what seemed an interminable wait at the cottage hospital, Maudie had been given a lift home in an ambulance going in her direction. It was en route to pick up a man who had slipped and fallen on his way home from the Royal Oak.

'Sounds like he has broken ribs,' the driver told Maudie, who was sitting beside him.

'It's funny he didn't call you sooner,' Maudie said. 'The pub must have closed hours ago.'

'According to his wife, she'd gone to bed early and didn't notice he was missing until she had to get up in the night to go to the lavatory. She got worried when she realized he hadn't come home, so she went out to look for him, and found him lying under a hedge, snoring fit to bust!'

'I trust he's not still lying there, then,

trying to catch pneumonia? Although that's what he richly deserves, staying out until all hours, getting drunk!'

'It seems she got a neighbour up and they managed to hoist the chap into a wheelbarrow and trundle him home, where they laid him out on a couch. When he came to he started hollering with the pain, and then the poor woman had to go out again to find a telephone. Aye, it's a great life if you don't weaken.'

'Tell me about it,' Maudie retorted. 'She's not the only one who has been up all night. What is the time, anyway?'

'Quarter to six,' the driver said, glancing at his wristwatch. 'I suppose when you get home you'll be able to sleep the day away, seeing as you don't work regular hours in your line of work? Lucky for some!'

*   *   *

The fire had died down when Maudie let herself into her cottage, but the place was still warm. The evening spent with Dick seemed to have happened a long time

120

ago. The dishes from their meal were still in the sink, but the water had seeped out, leaving food encrusted on the plates. Cleaning up would have to wait until later.

Peeling off her ruined stockings, which had now dried on her legs, she popped them into the ragbag. Yawning and stretching, she made her way upstairs. A hot bath was the order of the day, after which she would indulge herself in several slices of toast and Marmite and a cup of Horlicks. After that she would fall into her bed and . . .

There was a knock at the front door. Muttering to herself, Maudie lumbered back down the stairs and ripped the door open, to find the postman on the step.

'Morning, Nurse!'

'Morning, Fred. Do you have something for me?'

'Not at this time of day, Nurse. I'm just on my way to work. I've brought a message from my neighbour, Mrs Grant. The pains are coming every five minutes, she says. Real strong ones, too. You'd better come, she says.'

'Right. I'll get over there at once,' Maudie said, shutting the door in his face. She would have to apologize later for her rudeness, but just now she was in no mood for social niceties. Dragging herself wearily up the stairs, she put on her working gear and prepared for action. She reminded herself that she would need to stop at the parish hall to replenish the supplies in her bag. She groaned again when she opened the door of the coal shed, only to discover that her bicycle was missing. Of course, Dick had borrowed it, but where was it now? Left in a ditch where it could be stolen, she supposed. Now she would have to walk to the Grants' home and it was two miles each way.

'No rest for the wicked,' she told herself as she trudged down the road. She grinned suddenly, wondering what Miss Blythe would say to that. The silly woman would probably suggest that Maudie must have done something quite reprehensible in a past life, for which she had to pay this time around!

★   ★   ★

'Oh, it's you!' Maudie glared at the sight of Dick's cheerful face.

'Charming! Actually I've come to return your bike, but if this is a bad time I'll scarper.'

'I'm sorry, Dick. I'm having a rough day, that's all. Come through to the kitchen and I'll make us a cup of tea.'

'Oh? I've had visions of you sleeping all day after last night's little episode.'

'No such luck. I'd no sooner got home than I was called out again. I've been tied up all day with Mrs Grant's twins and I haven't been back long. Another five minutes and you wouldn't have found me opening the door because I'd have been in a well-deserved bath.'

'All well at the Grants' I hope?'

'Two lovely little boys, although the younger one of the pair is a bit puny. He'll bear watching until he puts on a bit of weight. He's not half the size of Greta's little chap.'

'Ah, now that's why am here. Apart from bringing back the bike, I mean.'

'The two of them are all right, I trust?'

'As far as I know, but I'm on the way to

123

question the girl about last night's accident.'

'What about the lad, then? Hasn't he come round yet?'

'Still unconscious, Sarge tells me. Anyway, I thought you might like to come with me, but I can see that you're all in.'

'No, no. I'd love to be there. You've brought the car; I can nap on the way. Can you wait while I put on a clean uniform? I'm afraid I'm looking a bit bedraggled.'

'I tell you what, Maudie. You dash up and have a quick bath, and I'll get rid of this lot while you're gone.' He indicated the previous evening's crockery, which still languished in the sink.

Maudie brightened up at once. 'Would you really? Now there's an offer I can't refuse.'

Delightedly, she bounded up the stairs, stopping halfway when a stabbing pain in her back reminded her that she was no longer a girl. Crouching over the Austin 7 in pouring rain had done her absolutely no good at all! Having limped into the bathroom, she threw an extra handful of bath salts into the tub and turned on the hot tap, praying that her temperamental geyser hadn't let her down as it sometimes did. Soon she was luxuriating in chin-deep water, and all was right with her world.

* * *

Maudie was surprised to find Greta's parents sitting at her bedside. Mrs Black pointed to the baby, sleeping peacefully in the wheeled cot nearby. 'Come to see little Frankie, then, have you, Nurse? Isn't he a lovely baby? He reminds me of our Greta at that age.'

'Frankie?' Maudie said, smiling. 'Short for Francis, I suppose.'

'That's right,' Greta said. 'I've called him after Dad.'

That was a clever move, Maudie thought, glancing at Frank Black, who looked slightly less glum than usual. Did this mean he'd changed his mind about his grandchild, now that the baby was here? If so, it would not be the first time that an unwanted child had thawed hard hearts with his innocent little being.

'I need to hear from you exactly what happened last night, Greta,' Dick said. 'Would you like your parents to wait outside while we talk?'

'There's nothing the girl could say that we shouldn't hear!' Frank growled. 'There's a few questions I'd like answers to myself!'

Mrs Black nodded encouragement to her daughter and Greta shrugged. 'Not much to tell. It was raining, see, and Matt said the roads were slippery. He's not all that used to driving, and when that horse suddenly ran into the road he had to stamp on the brakes and we ended up half in the ditch. I think we hit a milestone or something on the way.'

'I didn't know that Matt owned a car,' Maudie put in.

Greta shrugged again. 'Not exactly, he doesn't. Him and another chap have been restoring that old thing that belongs to their boss. It's as old as the hills, but the boss thought he could sell it when it was restored, and the lads would get some experience at fixing old cars at the same time.'

'So Matt took you for a little spin?' Dick said.

Greta tossed her head proudly. She'd copied the gesture from one of her precious film stars, Maudie realized. 'Oh, no. We were going to Gretna Green to get married.'

'What!' Frank Black roared. 'When I get my hands on that lad, I'll . . . '

But Maudie was just as dismayed as the irate father. 'How could you even think of doing such a thing?' she cried. 'To drive all that way in your condition, and so close to your time? What on earth did you think you were playing at?'

'Dad didn't leave us any choice!' Greta said. 'As it happened, we only got as far as Midvale when my pains started. I made Matt turn around and we were on our way home when the accident happened.'

'At least you had that much sense!'

Frank Black interrupted Maudie's little reprimand. She noted with some alarm that his red face warned of rising blood

127

pressure. 'A fine son-in-law that young idiot would have been. Can you wonder I refused to give my consent to the marriage? What will he be charged with, Constable? Possession of a stolen vehicle? Abduction of an under-age girl?'

'The car wasn't stolen, Dad!' Greta said. 'We only borrowed it. We would have taken it back after we came home from Scotland.'

'Would you, indeed! And what would Matt's boss have said to that, eh? More to the point, what's he going to say now, when he sees that great lump of twisted metal? And now I come to think about it, here's another charge for you, Constable: driving without insurance. I daresay the car wasn't covered for accidents because I understand it had been sitting abandoned in the man's back lot for ages until he decided it might be worth restoring.'

'A man in a coma can't be charged with anything,' Dick said. 'That will have to wait until he recovers consciousness — if he ever does.'

Greta broke into loud sobs, which

startled her baby, who in turn began to shriek. Mrs Black stared at her husband in disgust. 'Now see what you've done, you great lump!' she shouted, much to everyone's surprise.

15

After all the excitement of the past week, Maudie was thankful that life had settled down into a dull routine. The birthday party for little Ambrose Yolkowskie was a great success. A dozen small children crowded into the parish hall, all of them bearing gifts for the beaming little boy. Most of these treasures were small in size — a bar of chocolate or a rubber ball — but his evident delight at seeing his presents piled up on the table brought a lump to Maudie's throat. How pleased Helena must be with the way their fortunes had changed for the better, and all because of the safe arrival of her beautiful new daughter. And Maudie could take a little of the credit for that!

The mother of the birthday boy sat looking on, cradling little Barbara in her arms. She was unable to exchange more than a few words with the other women, but she made up for the lack with nods and smiles. Games were played under the direction of Mrs Blunt, who led the children in musical chairs, drop the handkerchief and Oranges and Lemons. Maudie's nursing skills came into play when the excitement proved too much for one ringleted child, who wet her knickers, but other than that there was nothing for her to do until it was time to feed the partygoers.

When the door opened she looked up, expecting to see Dick, who had promised to drop in if he could get away in time. A dark-haired man of middle height, wearing a shabby suit, hovered in the doorway. Maudie's heart sank. Surely this wasn't an expectant father? It would be just her luck if some poor woman passing through the district was about to give birth unexpectedly. She stood up, but before she could say anything young Ambrose detached himself from the ring of children and hurled himself on the man. Glancing over to where Helena sat, Maudie saw that the woman's face was alight with joy at the sight. This, then, must be Ambrose's father.

'Isn't it marvellous?' Mrs Blunt enthused. 'I'm so glad he got here in time! Harold had a word with that Polish chap at the farm, and we managed to contact Josef at his digs in Cardiff. I'm told that he's had no luck finding a job as yet, but at least he knows now that his wife is safe and well after the birth of their daughter.'

'Yes, indeed,' Maudie said, delighted to watch this family reunion.

'Come along, everybody!' Mrs Blunt called, clapping her hands. 'We'll have a game of Ring a Ring of Roses, and then it will be time to have tea!'

The door opened again, and this time it was Dick who came in, carrying a large cardboard box. 'What on earth have you got in there?' Maudie asked. 'Something for the church jumble sale?'

'It's my old train set,' Dick told her, lifting the lid slightly so she could see inside. 'I'm giving it to the little boy.'

'You've kept it all these years!' she marvelled.

'Yes, well, I never could bear to give it up. I've always thought I'd have a son of my own to pass it on to, but that hasn't happened, so Ambrose may as well have the use of it.'

'But you still might,' Maudie said. 'Have a son of your own, I mean.' Dick was only forty-five and there was still time for him to marry and start a family. She could imagine him sprawling on a hearthrug, showing a tiny replica of himself how to fit the metal tracks together. With a pang, she realized that the scenario would have to include a wife and mother. There would be no room for Maudie there.

'Oh, no, I shan't have a son,' Dick said firmly. He didn't elaborate on this, and she wondered what he meant, but she didn't like to ask. As a nurse, she wondered if there was some sort of hereditary disease in his family that he couldn't risk passing on.

Grace was said, and the delighted children attacked the food. Maudie stared in horrified fascination at an awful child who kept up a running conversation with his mouth wide open, displaying half-masticated cake.

Dick was equally spellbound. 'Somebody needs to learn some table manners,' he grunted. 'Has his mother never told him not to eat and talk at the same time?'

The food disappeared in a hurry, but it appeared that the awful child wasn't satisfied. He reached out and snatched half a fairy cake from his neighbour's plate and rammed it into his mouth. Under cover of the ensuing uproar, Maudie left for home, with Dick in tow.

'Don't forget the meeting tonight!' Mrs Blunt hissed. Maudie waved a hand in response.

'I say, I haven't had a chance to give the youngster his train set,' Dick said. 'I'll have to go back in. What's the big rush?'

'I'm an old hand at these things,' Maudie told him. 'I know what's going to happen next. That over-stuffed boy will vomit all over the floor, and guess who'll be expected to mop it up? Nurse Rouse, of course! Isn't that what nurses do? Yes, you go back and do what you have to do, but take a tip from me. Don't let the children see what's in that box of yours, or you'll never get rid of them. Come to my place when you're finished, and we'll have a good old natter.'

'How are your twins getting along? Is the smaller one holding his own?' Dick asked, when they were back at Maudie's cottage. She had opened all the windows and the sweet spring air was blowing in, bringing with it the scent of wallflowers.

'He's managed to put on an ounce or two,' Maudie said. 'I think he'll do. The only problem is that his parents are fighting over what names to give the boys.'

'Being twins, I suppose they want names beginning with the same letter,' Dick remarked. 'Peter and Paul, say, or Ronald and Richard.'

'If only it were so sensible,' Maudie groaned. 'Now the parents have decided that they'll each choose a name for one of the boys. Mrs Grant wants Albert, after her late father.'

'Nothing wrong with that! If it was good enough for Queen Victoria it's good enough for Baby Grant.'

'Ah, but wait until you hear what Thomas Grant has in mind for the other one. Ulysses, of all things!'

'What on earth . . . '

'Apparently there was an American president called Ulysses Grant, at the time of their Civil War. Thomas read about him in the *Boys' Own Paper* when he was a child, and convinced himself they are related.'

'And are they?'

'I very much doubt it. Grant is a popular name, and they can't all be connected, can they?'

'Luckily we don't have to worry about that sort of thing,' Dick said, stretching his arms above his head. 'Albert and Ulysses, indeed!'

'Now that's where you're wrong! The pair of them have reached a compromise of sorts. They say they want me to choose the name, and they insist they'll abide by my decision.'

'Ouch!'

'Exactly. And I'll need the wisdom of Solomon to deal with it. And what if the Grants don't like the names I've chosen?'

'Oh, I don't know. There is a way around this. Give the boys plain, sensible names they won't be ashamed of, or they'll get teased about it at school. John and James, say. Tack on the ones their parents are keen on as second names; they can always drop those in later years.'

'You may have something there. How about John Ulysses and James Albert?'

'It could be a lot worse,' Dick agreed, pleased with his solution.

It struck Maudie that they sounded like parents themselves, engaged in the happy task of naming a cherished new arrival. She had always been more than contented with her lot and had never hankered after marriage and children. Now, sitting beside Dick in happy companionship, she was beginning to think she'd missed something.

16

'You've named him *what?*' Mrs Blunt's eyebrows had risen dramatically. 'How could you, Nurse? It's hardly a Christian name, is it? In fact, I'm not sure that Harold will agree to baptize the baby with a name like that.'

'He can't find anything wrong with John,' Maudie pointed out. 'There was John the Baptist, for a start. And the other twin's name will be James. When he came up with the idea, Dick said he was reminded of the Apostles James and John, the sons of Zebedee, and he knows his Bible, does Dick. Come to think of it, Albert isn't in the holy writ either, but I know of at least two Alberts the vicar has christened over the years.'

'If you say so, Nurse. Oh, dear! Why are people so slow in turning up for this meeting? I'd like to get started this side of midnight, if possible.'

The purpose of the meeting was to

finalize plans for the church fête. Maudie was there because she didn't want to get drafted for some boring job in her absence. Ideally she'd like to be in charge of the first aid tent, but probably that plum job would go to Pratt, the sexton, who had trained with the St John's Ambulance brigade.

Slowly the interested parties filed in, taking their seats as far as possible from other participants, as if they feared contamination from those with opposing views. Dr Dean strolled in and took a seat in the back row. Now why was he here? Surely he wasn't about to volunteer to man the first aid tent? That would be far beneath him, as a doctor with such a high opinion of himself.

Miss Blythe came next. Maudie stared in admiration at the woollen cape the woman was wearing. It was a glorious mixture of bottle-green and deep purple. It looked expensive. Not for the first time, Maudie wondered where Miss Blythe got her money. The Royal Oak wasn't exactly the Ritz, yet it did cost money to stay there. Did she have private means?

Frank Black entered, looking belligerent. Maudie guessed that he wanted to assert his authority here, having failed miserably over the issue of baby Frankie. Paul Allen followed. That was another man who tried to rule his household with a rod of iron, as Maudie knew well.

At last, when the hall was almost full, Mrs Blunt rose, calling the meeting to order. She began by tendering the apologies of the vicar, who was 'unavoidably detained'. Maudie grinned. She knew what that meant. He was skulking at home, hoping to avoid the conflicts that were bound to arise.

Frank Black was quickly on his feet. 'Is this fête really necessary? That's what I want to know. It's nothing but a lot of turmoil and disruption, with a mess to be cleared up afterwards.'

'It is if you don't want to get rained on in church one of these Sundays,' the sexton called out. 'This event is in aid of the roof fund.'

'Get away with you!' another man shouted. 'That roof's been on St John's for centuries. It won't give way in my time, or yours!'

'Please, gentlemen!' Mrs Blunt rapped on the table with her gavel. 'The decision to hold the fête has already been made by the vestry committee. We are here tonight to decide on what the attractions will be, and who will take charge of them.'

'I'm sorry, madam, but I will have my say!' Frank Black was not so easily crushed. 'It's like this. It's not just a question of turning up and standing behind the white elephant stall, you know! We're all being asked to donate prizes for this and that, and the women give their jams and home baking and knitted goods. All that costs good money before we ever turn up on the day. Now I'm not saying it isn't right to support the church. My idea is this. Just give the amount of money we would have laid out, but avoid all the aggravation that goes with the fête.'

There were a few mutters of 'hear, hear' and Mrs Blunt, who had steered the Mothers' Union through many a crisis, hastened to rally her troops. Maudie listened with half an ear as her friend described the ways in which additional revenue would come from people not connected to the parish, who would turn out to enjoy a day of lighthearted fun.

'I do so agree!' Miss Blythe called. 'I have heard from my sister, who will be back in England in time to come along to join us. Madam Zora can see into the future! If you cross her palm with silver she will read your palm or peer into the crystal ball on your behalf. For an extra sixpence she will even consult the tarot cards.'

'I might have a go at that myself,' Maudie muttered, looking back over her shoulder at Dr Dean. 'Maybe Madam Zora can tell me how to cope with his nibs back there.'

As if he had read her mind, Dr Dean raised his hand. 'I shall need a table in a sheltered spot, preferably in a tent,' he announced. 'For those of you who don't yet know me, I'm Dr Donald Dean. You'll be seeeing a lot of me in future because I've bought into Dr Mallory's practice.' This provoked an excited buzz as people took in this information. 'It occurs to me that this fête of yours will be a good place for me to explain the ramifications of the new National Health Service,' he went on. 'I shall have pamphlets to hand out, and I'll be pleased to answer any questions that people may have.'

Maudie admitted to herself that it sounded like a good idea, despite what she felt about the personality of the doctor. There was a great deal of confusion about the scheme and people weren't sure what to believe. The chance to get dental treatment, spectacles, prescriptions, and consultations with specialists, all free of charge, sounded much too good to be true. On the other hand, the newspapers had been full of angry letters from doctors who opposed the scheme. Who were you supposed to believe? Perhaps the National Health Service wasn't such a good idea after all. As an insider, Maudie knew something of what the doctors' scepticism was about. Why should highly skilled medical personnel be dictated to by politicians who knew very little about how the profession worked?

'An excellent idea,' Mrs Blunt said. 'I shall see that a table is set up for you in the first aid tent, Doctor.'

Maudie suppressed a giggle. It was obvious that Dr Dean had never practiced in a rural community before, or he would have run a mile before he'd willingly lay himself open to meet all comers! Now he would find himself fielding all sorts of questions that had nothing to do with the provisions of the Health Act. She predicted a long queue of people seeking miracle cures for everything from bunions to constipation. She hoped he was up to the task.

Mrs Blunt consulted her list. 'Next, the Beautiful Baby competition. We need a judge for that. How about you, Nurse Rouse? If anybody knows about babies, you do.'

'What!' Maudie yelped. 'Oh, no, not me! I couldn't possibly do it! Think about the mothers of all the babies who didn't win a prize. They'd never speak to me again, and I do have to work here, you know.' She paused. 'I have a wonderful idea! Why don't we ask Dr Dean to do the judging? He's the real expert here and nobody could possibly question his decision.' She turned to face the doctor. 'I'd be honoured to hand out the literature for you, Dr Dean. After all, that doesn't take any particular skill, does it?'

Preening himself like a peacock surrounded by a harem of peahens, the doctor graciously agreed to do the job. Maudie smiled like a crocodile eying a missionary. Mrs Blunt looked at her through narrowed eyes.

★ ★ ★

It was not until much later — long after the murder had occurred, in fact — that Maudie looked back on this meeting and realized that all the signs had been there. Signs, that was, that someone had planned to kill and had ruthlessly carried out a campaign to make sure that they could get away with it.

Had she not been so worried about being turned out of her cottage and perhaps losing her means of livelihood, she might possibly have noticed something odd and put two and two together, but that she had failed to do. And, to do her justice, she had been busy enough bringing new babies into the world, without worrying overmuch about people who might be ushered out of it, whether by fair means or foul.

To keep herself sane she had to keep other people's problems at bay, although it was hard to do when she was so intimately tied to their lives. There was the teenager, Greta Black, with a baby, a stern father and a young man who lay unconscious in the cottage hospital. Clarice Allen, a young mother suffering from post-partum depression. The Yolkowskies and their little family, trying to survive in a disused railway carriage. Young Lily Willis, faced with the prospect of being shipped off to Australia for a reunion with a birth mother she could no longer remember.

Maudie felt ashamed. She had her problems, yet there were so many people who were much worse off. She was strong and healthy; even if she were forced to give up midwifery she was bound to find work somewhere. She remembered her childhood ambition, to work in a sweetie shop. Well, there were worse fates that could befall a woman!

'I think that will be all for this evening,' Mrs Blunt said, jerking Maudie's mind back to the present.

The scraping of chairs on the wooden floor heralded the departure of the good parishioners of St. John's Church. Outside, the moon shone down on Llandyfan, and all seemed right with the world.

17

Maudie woke up with a feeling of well-being. It had rained in the night, but now a mist was rising from the fields near her cottage, bringing with it the promise of good weather to come. She was looking forward to spending the afternoon at the church fête, which promised all the simple pleasures of a village holiday. She was glad that it would not be spoiled by cold and damp conditions.

Although the event didn't officially begin until after lunch, she decided to walk over to see what progress was being made in setting up. The fête was being held in the glebe, a piece of land owned by the church. Being conveniently located, it was often used for school sports days and village cricket.

Maudie took her best summer dress out of mothballs, looking at it with satisfaction. The navy blue fabric was speckled with a pattern of daisies in pale

148

blue, mauve and white. It delighted her now as much as it had done before the war, when she had spotted it in a shop window and gone inside to put a deposit of half a crown on it. She had paid off the rest in weekly installments until at last she was able to carry it home in triumph. Yes, the dress was most attractive. As to style, however, it was nothing like Christian Dior's 'New Look' that the designer had launched last year. She had seen pictures of Princess Margaret on the newsreel at the cinema, wearing the full-skirted frocks and coats that were all the rage. Maudie's garment was much more basic — but then, so were nurses' salaries.

She gave her glossy hair one hundred strokes with the hairbrush, frowning at herself in the mirror. Dare she go out wearing her hair loose on her shoulders? Perhaps Llandyfan's matrons would regard that as being too youthful a style for a woman in her forties. Should she get it cut short for the summer? The problem there was that a nurse's hair must never touch her collar, and Maudie knew from past experience that too short a cut didn't suit her. She felt it made her face look like a peeled banana. She sighed and bundled up the hair into a chignon that was a bit more elegant than its usual bun.

Strolling down the street, she stopped in front of a neighbour's garden to admire a rose that had the most glorious scent. She didn't know the Davises well; they were newcomers to the village who had settled in shortly after the war. The husband was a clerk who worked for the local council; his wife was a housewife who sometimes came to Women's Institute meetings.

The sound of raised voices came to Maudie's ears. Unwilling to disturb their privacy, she was about to move on when she heard an unmistakable sound. Somebody had smashed a piece of crockery, which pointed to escalating violence.

Opening the garden gate, she trotted towards the house, calling, 'Cooee!' as she came. The loud voices continued. She tapped on the kitchen door. After a moment it was flung open by Mr Davis, who glared at Maudie.

'Yes? What is it?'

'Is everything all right here?' she asked.

He grunted. 'Apart from the wife getting hysterical over nothing! I suppose it's that men's paws thing you hear about. Foolish old women having fits over every little thing!'

'I am not having the menopause, Graham Davis!' His wife appeared at the door, red-faced. 'Hello, Nurse! Can I help you?'

'I was just passing on my way to the fête,' Maudie mumbled, 'and I wondered if there was anything I could do to help.' She didn't know what the couple would make of that meaningless statement, but she wasn't a policeman. She could hardly say she was worried that their argument might lead to blows.

'Help!' the woman cried. 'Not unless you can bake and ice a cake before two o'clock, with no ingredients to do it with. Come inside and have a look at this!'

A fine chocolate cake held pride of place on the kitchen table. Someone had cut out a large slice and it was apparent that the cake had been made in three layers, held together with butter icing. Maudie's gaze went to the linoleum floor, where shards of china lat scattered, adorned with cake crumbs.

'Yes, you may well stare, Nurse!' Mrs Davis snapped. 'I baked that cake specially for the fête, and do you see what that great lummox did?'

'I've a right to eat what I like in my own home,' Davis said. 'I pay for the stuff to make it, don't I?' Tears sprang to his wife's eyes.

'Why don't you go away and leave us to it?' Maudie told him. 'I can help to sort this out, I'm sure.'

'Don't you tell me what to do in my own home!' he blustered.

Maudie looked him straight in the eye. 'Then I suggest you go quietly, Mr Davis, or I shall have to ring 999.'

For a moment it seemed that he would defy her; but then, with an outraged snort, he banged out of the room.

'Come and sit down, Mrs Davis,' Maudie said. 'Would it help if I made you a cup of tea?' The woman would be within her rights to echo her husband's sentiments about being dictated to in their own house, but the two women were nurse and patient now. Comfort was needed and Maudie was here to give it.

'No, no, I'm all right, Nurse, but oh! My poor cake! I'm in charge of the cake stall, you see, and this here was supposed to be the focal point. It's my own fault, I suppose. I've boasted about this marvellous recipe I clipped from a magazine and now I've nothing to show for it. I can't bear it if people think I'm a fool or a liar!'

'You could donate it to the tea tent,' Maudie suggested. 'Sell it at so much a slice.'

'It wouldn't be the same at all,' Mrs Davis cried. Maudie thought again. Then her eyes brightened. 'I know what we'll do. We'll have a competition, with a prize for the best cake.'

'I don't know what you mean.'

'I'll have a word with Mrs Blunt, but I'm sure she'll agree to it. It will be easy enough to organize, with you in charge of that stall. We'll find someone to judge the baking and of course a slice will have to be removed from each cake for the judge to taste. After that, the cakes can be sold as planned, and if yours wins you'll be able to charge a bit over the top when it goes.'

'I don't know . . . ' Mrs Davis began.

Maudie shrugged. 'It's up to you, of course, but if you want me to speak to Mrs Blunt, now's your chance.'

'Oh, I suppose so, Nurse. Who will you ask to judge the cakes?'

'One of the men, probably. Women are usually too worried about their waistlines to want to eat a lot of cake.'

Maudie went on her way, conscious of a job well done. At this rate she'd make a good candidate for the municipal elections, although if a woman were to be voted in it would be a first for Llandyfan, where old prejudices still prevailed.

She found Mrs Blunt in the rectory kitchen, making sandwiches. 'You won't mind if I carry on with this, will you, Nurse? I want to leave something for Harold's lunch before I go over to see what's happening in the tea tent. And there are boxes to unpack with things for the white elephant stall. So much to do!'

'I can help with that,' Maudie said. 'The unpacking, I mean. Otherwise I shan't have much to do until after the official opening. Now, let me tell you why I've come.'

Mrs Blunt listened carefully to what Maudie had to say, all the while spreading mustard on thin slices of ham. 'Oh, that silly man! Where has he been all these weeks while we've been making plans for this fête? Your idea is a good compromise, Nurse, but whom shall we ask to judge the cakes? All the churchwardens are already spoken for, running the children's races and the men's tug of war and so on.'

'I have the very man!' Maudie said. 'Dick Bryant had been assigned to keep an eye on the fête, just in case there was any problem with rambunctious youth.'

* * *

As she neared the glebe Maudie caught sight of a woman in the distance, hurrying in the same direction. She recognized Miss Blythe's glorious green and purple cape, although why the woman should choose to wear such a heavy garment on a warm June day was anyone's guess. She had the hood up, too.

Maudie forgot all about the woman when she entered the field, which was buzzing with activity. Not a single box had been opened at the white elephant table, and nobody seemed to know who was meant to be in charge. She donned her apron and set to work.

When a shadow fell over the table she looked up, smiling, anticipating Dick's arrival. Instead, Dr Dean loomed over her as she straightened up from her task. He was smartly dressed in an expensive-looking suit, with one of those ties that proclaims its wearer to be the graduate of some distinguished institution. She thought that his outfit was more suited to a garden party than a village fête. The other men were wearing flannel bags and cricketing pullovers, or similarly casual attire.

'Good morning, Nurse.' His tone was cold as his eyes raked her from head to toe. Really, she thought, he couldn't be more disgusted if I was wearing one of those new-fangled bikini bathing costumes!

'Is that what you intend to wear this afternoon, Nurse? Where is your uniform?'

'My uniform?' she stammered. 'I don't know what you mean, Doctor.'

'Surely that should be obvious, Nurse. You will be representing me, by handing out literature. This a professional engagement and it calls for a professional attitude.'

Behind her back, Maudie's hands clenched into fists. Steady, old girl! she warned herself. She put on her sweetest smile. 'I have a message for you from Mrs Blunt,' she told him.

'Is that so? Am I being let off from judging that ridiculous baby contest?'

'Actually, she was hoping you might assist in another capacity as well. Mrs Blunt would like you to judge the best cake competition. It has to be someone who is new to the village, you see. Every other man here has an interest in the outcome of this because his wife will have entered a cake.' This was a gross exaggeration, but Maudie was determined to have her way. If Dr Dean thought he could bully her, he had another thing coming! He would meet his match, word for word and blow for blow.

18

That afternoon found Maudie on the job, still wearing her pretty cotton frock. A charabanc had come from Midvale, disgorging the local brass band in their smart red and yellow uniforms. It was pleasant to be sitting out of doors while lively music wafted in her direction from the other end of the field.

'Hello, Nurse. What have you got here, then?'

Maudie smiled and handed a pamphlet to the elderly man standing in front of her. Of course everyone knew who she was; it simply wasn't necessary for her to be wearing uniform on her day off.

'Have one of these, Mr Ransome. It explains all about the new health service.'

He opened his mouth in a toothless grin. 'Aye, I can't wait for the day they give me new choppers,' he told her. 'First thing I'm going to do is eat a great big steak!'

'Chance would be a fine thing,' Maudie told him. Meat had been rationed since 1940. 'There are some lovely cakes for sale over there, though. Why don't you go and take a look?' He should be able to gum on a slice of Mrs Davis's chocolate cake if he managed to purchase it.

Daisy Larke came by, pushing her baby in a shabby pram.

'Hello, Daisy! How is little Richard? Did you enter him in the beautiful baby competition?' Maudie tickled the child under the chin.

Daisy's expression darkened. 'Yes I did, and I wish I hadn't. Honestly, that doctor! Who does he think he is?'

'Why, what did he do?'

'Oh, he only said Richard is too fat! It isn't healthy for a child to put on too much weight, he says. I should let him spend an hour a day on the floor, exercising his limbs! My Richard isn't fat! He's chubby, and everyone admires a chubby baby! Who's Mummy's little pet, then? We don't like that nasty doctor, do we?'

'Oh, just ignore him,' Maudie said.

'Listen, isn't that the 'Merry Widow Waltz' they're playing? I think I'll have a wander round for a bit. Nobody else seems to want a pamphlet at the moment.'

She admired the ingenuity of Mrs Blunt and the parish council, who had put on this fête despite the difficulties posed by post-war restrictions. She was amazed to see in operation that old stand-by of village fête, a coconut shy. Of course real coconuts could not be had for love nor money, but the indefatigable Mrs Blunt had substituted turnips, and instead of wooden balls the competitors were hurling beanbags borrowed from the village school. Prizes were awarded to anyone who succeeded in dislodging a turnip, although, Maudie reflected, there was a time not long past when people would have been delighted to win a turnip to take home for the pot.

Another disgruntled mother stopped Maudie in front of the second-hand bookstall. 'Who does that doctor think he is?'

'Has he said your Larry is too fat?'

'No. He's too pale, if you please! I'm suppose to give him an airing every day, never mind he sits out in the pram whenever the weather's fine.'

'Take no notice, Mrs Barnes,' Maudie murmured. 'Larry has inherited your lovely complexion, that's all.'

When the woman had moved on, Maudie indulged in a little giggle. Another unhappy customer, she thought. He's supposed to be running a beautiful baby contest, not a clinic.

Dr Dean had a lot to learn if he intended to practice in a rural area. The trick to running a baby contest was to compliment every parent on some aspect of the child's appearance. It was always possible to find something good to say about the homeliest contestant: pretty hair, fine teeth, sturdy limbs or sparkling eyes. If the man applied his ill-conceived methods when he judged the cakes, he would have a riot on his hands. The women of Llandyfan were justly proud of their baking skills, and pity the man who rushed in where angels feared to tread!

Oh, there was Dick! The men's tug of

war had just been announced, and it looked as if he'd been roped in to act as referee. A photographer from the *Midvale Chronicle*, whose task it was to photograph the winning baby, now moved over to get a shot of the action. Men in shirtsleeves prepared to do battle.

Maudie moved closer to see what was going on. The event was a demonstration match between the cricketers and the lawn bowlers. With weary resignation, she noticed that the St John's Ambulance man, who was supposed to be in charge of the first aid tent, had moved into line in support of the lawn bowlers. That meant that Maudie might be called upon to administer first aid for any resulting bumps and bruises. Unless, of course, Dr Dean decided to elbow his way in.

She badly needed a cold drink, but the queue at the tea tent was too long for her liking, so she walked on. She noticed that the door of the striped tent where Madam Zora was supposed to be telling fortunes was fastened shut, with a notice hanging from one of the guy lines. 'Closed', it read.

'That's funny,' Maudie said to herself. Surely this was the time of day when business would be brisk. As she stood staring at the tent two teenaged girls approached her, nudging each other and giggling.

'Are you her?' one asked.

'I beg your pardon?'

'The fortune-teller. Madam Zora. Where is she? We've waited ever such a long time to see her, but she's never come.'

'No, I'm not Madam Zora,' Maudie told her. Obviously these were visitors from outside the village, or they would have known who she was. 'I expect she's gone for a cup of tea or something.'

The girl shook her head. 'We've been here ever so many times and we haven't seen anyone going in. I bet she never came at all. This is so disappointing! We came to see her special-like. It costs money to travel on a bus, you know!' She looked at Maudie accusingly.

'I should try again later,' Maudie told her, 'unless you want me to tell your fortune for you.'

The second girl looked at her eagerly.

164

'Can you see into the future, then?'

'Oh yes. Very often I can, but I'm afraid I can't help you today. I have a job to do here.' She walked away, leaving them gaping after her.

Yes, she could see into their future all right. These silly girls would want to know about glamorous jobs and prospective boyfriends, of course, and as a midwife she knew only too well where that might lead. Greta Black's head had been turned by the Hollywood fantasies she'd seen at the cinema, and just look at her now!

★   ★   ★

Maudie had not been back at her table for very long when the air was rent with loud screams. She ignored the interruption while she advised a man on suitable treatment for the rope burns on his hands, but the screams kept coming. She frowned. Why was nobody dealing with the problem, whatever it was? Dick Bryant was on the grounds, as was the doctor. Let someone else take charge for once.

The two teenagers she'd spoken to previously flung themselves into the first aid tent, clutching each other and howling.

'What on earth is the matter with you two?' Maudie demanded. 'Do stop that screeching, child! Have you seen a ghost?'

'It's her, Miss!' one of them panted. 'Madam Zora. She's dead!' The girl broke into a fresh volley of sobs.

'Dead? Try to calm down and tell me what you're talking about.' It could be stuffy in a small tent with the door closed. Perhaps the woman had been overcome with the heat and fainted.

'We thought she might be inside her tent, so we undid the door and had a look. It was awful, miss. She's lying with her face on the table and there's a great big knife sticking out of her back!'

'What's going on here?' Maudie was relieved to hear Dick's calm voice.

'Oh, Constable! I'm so glad you're here,' she murmured. 'It seems there's been a murder.'

19

Dick took charge in his usual capable manner. One man was dispatched to fetch Dr Dean; another to phone police headquarters from the rectory. The two girls were placed in the care of a capable onlooker, and warned not to leave the fête.

Maudie flew across to the fortune-tellers's tent before anyone could stop her. She wanted to see for herself what had taken place.

'Don't go in there, Maudie, it's a crime scene,' Dick warned, but she knew better than to interfere with what must be a gory spectacle. Instead she stopped in the doorway, peering through the flap the girls had left open. As they had reported, Madam Zara lay face down on the iron table that had held her crystal ball. In the gloom Maudie could just make out the hilt of a knife protruding from the poor woman's back, but that was all. Any blood there might be was not visible from the entrance.

She took a careful look around the tent but there wasn't much to see in the tiny space. The crystal ball, apparently dislodged when the killer struck, had rolled into the corner. Didn't the woman have a handbag? Maudie couldn't spot one, but it might be hidden from view. The table was covered with a red chenille tablecloth, made for a much larger piece of furniture, so that its fringed edges swept the grass.

What struck her as strange was the garment that was suspended from the tent pole. Not that there was anything odd about it as such; it was a very nice cloak. It was just that the thing belonged to Miss Myrtle Blythe. So what was it doing here?

Don't be making mysteries where none exist, Maudie chided herself. Madam Zora was Miss Blythe's sister. It wasn't outside the bounds of possibility that the two women owned identical cloaks. The pair might have a similar taste in clothing, and while it might seem strange for two elderly women to dress in identical garments, that would not have been a problem here. They did not live near each other, and in fact Madam Zora had been abroad until recently.

'I must stop calling her that,' Maudie said aloud. 'She must have a proper name; nobody goes around calling herself Madam Zora!'

'When you've finished talking to yourself I'll need you to help me,' Dick said, coming up behind Maudie.

'Me? What can I do? Look for people with blood on their hands?'

'This is no joking matter, Nurse Rouse.'

'No, sorry, of course it isn't. I'm just a bit rattled, I suppose. What do you want me to do?'

'First of all, see if you can find Miss Blythe. I don't want her to hear the bad news in passing. In fact, if she is not here, I may want you to come with me when we go to break the news to her at the Royal Oak.'

'I'm sure that she was here, Dick. At least . . . '

'What is it?'

Well, I thought I saw her in the lane earlier. She has a very distinctive cape and she was wearing that today. In fact, it's hanging in the tent at this moment. Only, now I wonder . . . '

'If the victim was wearing her sister's coat.'

'That's just it. Unless of course both the sisters own similar capes.'

'Right. Well, off you go then, if you don't mind. See if you can find the poor old girl. This is going to come as a terrible shock to her.'

On her way across to the tea tent, she encountered Mrs Blunt, who seemed more distressed than Maudie had ever seen her. 'Oh, Nurse! This is an absolute disaster! I know I shouldn't be concerned with money when some poor soul has been killed, but we shan't make a thing here today and everyone has worked so hard to make the fête a success. I suppose there's no mistake about this? Madam Zora didn't have a sudden heart attack or something?'

'She was stabbed, I'm afraid.'

'Oh, dear! And now I suppose the police will want to keep everybody here for questioning, and people will be mumbling and grumbling and blaming it all on us.'

'At least the reporter from the Chronicle will be delighted. I can imagine the head-lines now: *Murder in the Glebe by our reporter on the spot*.'

'I suppose it will make a change from writing about who won the various races and whatnot,' Mrs Blunt said gloomily. 'I must make sure he takes note of all those details before he gets carried away with the murder story.'

'Speaking of which, who won the beautiful baby contest?'

Mrs Blunt wrinkled her nose. 'A golden-haired little moppet from Mid-vale. A budding Shirley Temple, by the look of her. She smiled up at the dear doctor and I suppose he couldn't resist her. Perhaps it's just as well that nobody from our village won, or half of our young mothers wouldn't be speaking to each other. I don't think we'll have one of these contests again. It causes too much turmoil in the all round.'

'Speaking of which,' Maudie said, 'here comes the good doctor now.'

Dr Dean approached them, looking rather rumpled. 'Is it true what I hear, Nurse? There's been a death?'

'Yes, Doctor. I say, you look a little damp! Would you like me to fetch you a towel?'

'One of the little brutes wet on me,' he snapped. 'Now I shall have to get this suit dry-cleaned. Don't ask me to judge one of these wretched competitions again, Nurse! They are more trouble than they're worth!'

'That's just what we were saying, Doctor,' Maudie agreed. 'Now then, just continue along here and you'll see the fortune-teller's tent. It's the seer who has been stabbed.'

'This place is a madhouse,' he complained.

* * *

Miss Blythe was nowhere to be found, and it was quite some time before

Maudie and Dick were able to meet her at the Royal Oak. Following the arrival of the police inspector and his team, Dick was kept busy taking down names and addresses of people who might be interviewed later, although many of the young children and their parents were allowed to leave right away.

Mrs Blunt and her helpers were faced with the task of packing up all the unsold items from the book and white elephant stalls. Once word of the murder had leaked out, people were far more interested in crowding close to the crime scene than thumbing through second-hand Penguins and looking at mismatched china.

'What are you going to do with all this?' Maudie wondered.

'Oh, we'll have a mammoth jumble sale in the parish hall some day soon, I should think. At least all the edibles have gone. That's one good thing about having had a war. People are so used to being deprived, they're willing to pounce on any extra good food that comes their way.'

'Shame! I wanted to get my hands on that chocolate cake.'

'Then you missed a treat, because it won the grand prize!'

'Then I did something right today for change.'

'What do you mean?'

'Never mind. Patient confidentiality,' Maudie said.

'I see,' Mrs Blunt replied, not seeing at all.

* * *

'Is it true what I've heard?' Len Frost, landlord of the Royal Oak, looked up from polishing glasses when Dick and Maudie walked in. 'Some chaps came in for a drink and said they'd been at the church do and heard there'd been a stabbing there. They had to provide their names and addresses for the police, they said, in case they need to be interviewed later.'

'Yes, it's true enough,' Dick said.

'Fancy that! Who was it, then, some poor chap who just dropped in for a look-see and got himself stabbed by some yobbos?'

'I'm afraid it's worse than that, Len. It was Miss Blythe's sister.'

'Never!'

'Nurse and I have come to break the news. Is Miss Blythe upstairs now?'

'Far as I know. Do you want the wife to go up with you, for a bit of moral support, like?'

'That won't be necessary. Nurse will help me.'

'Right you are, then. You know the way up to the guest rooms, Nurse.'

Indeed Maudie did. Only last year she had attended the sickbed there of a man who had turned out to be a murderer. This time, of course, there was no question of anything like that.

Miss Blythe opened the door in response to their knock. 'Oh, it's you two!' she sniffed. 'What do you want?'

'May we come in, madam?'

'It's really not very convenient at the moment. I was just about to take a bath.'

'I'm sorry. I'm afraid this won't wait. I'm sorry to have to tell you, madam, that your sister has been found dead.'

20

Miss Blythe stared at them as if turned to stone. Maudie took her gently by the arm and steered her back into the bedroom, leaving it to Dick to close the door behind them.

'Would you like to lie down, Miss Blythe?'

'I don't know what you mean.' The older woman sat down suddenly on the bedside chair, holding her hands in front of her as if trying to ward off unseen perils.

'It's the shock,' Maudie told Dick. 'She can't quite take it in.'

'I suppose we could come back later,' he said, 'but she shouldn't be left alone in this state. Do you think we should call the doctor? He might want to prescribe a sedative.'

'No doctors!' Miss Blythe shouted, making them both jump. 'I've had enough of them. Never again! What I want is police protection! I insist that you stay here with me, Constable!'

Maudie frowned. This seemed a step too far. Informed that her sister was dead, Miss Blythe had uttered no word of regret or denial, either of which might have been natural given the circumstances. Instead, she seemed to assume that she would be the next victim. Was there a homicidal maniac intent upon wiping out the whole Blythe family, one by one? It hardly seemed likely.

'Why do you feel you need special protection, Madam?' Dick asked gently. Miss Blythe glared at him as if the answer was obvious to anyone of minimal intelligence.

'Surely you haven't forgotten how I was pushed into the river, Constable? And just what are you people doing to find out who did that, may I ask? It seems to me that you have made no attempt whatsoever to bring the criminal to book!'

Dick ran his finger around the inside of his collar. Maudie felt sorry for him. She knew that his superiors had dismissed Miss Blythe's claims as the dotty ramblings of an elderly person who had simply slipped on wet grass. Dick cleared his throat. 'I don't really think that the two events are connected, Miss Blythe.'

'How am I going to convince you, man? Someone tried to drown me the other day, and now Octavia is dead!

'Yes, madam, and I'm very sorry indeed for your loss. Rest assured the police will do everything in their power to find the person or persons who killed your sister.'

'But can't you see? It wasn't Octavia they wanted out of the way. It was me! She was wearing my cape when she went to the fête today. Everyone knows that cape of mine, and everyone knows that I'm staying here at the Royal Oak. When Octavia left here somebody followed, thinking they were stalking me.'

Startled, Maudie interrupted the pair. 'But why was she wearing your cape?'

'She was in fancy dress for her Madam Zora role. She didn't want to be seen in public wearing those garments; she said that would destroy the mystery. She wanted the clients' first glimpse of her to be inside the tent, sitting at the table with her crystal ball. Oh, that ball she had was just window-dressing, you know. There's nothing magical about it; just ordinary glass.'

Maudie nodded. So the woman she had seen wending her way to the glebe — how long ago that seemed — had been Octavia. The distinctive cape had led Maudie to believe she was seeing Myrtle Blythe, and perhaps the killer had fallen into the same trap.

A tap at the door interrupted her train of thought. Dick opened it to reveal Dora Frost, the landlord's wife. 'I'm sorry to interrupt, Dick, but there's a Dr Dean downstairs. He's come to take a look at Miss Blythe. Shall I show him up?'

'I have no wish to see a doctor!' Miss Blythe snapped.

'I'm sorry, madam, but when we heard of your tragic loss my husband felt it best to send for the doctor. We heard he was up at the fête, so he didn't have far to come.'

'Yes, please send him up,' Dick said, and in due course Miss Blythe submitted

most ungraciously to the doctor's minis-
trations. Maudie didn't think much of his
bedside manner, either, but she was
thankful that he had put in an appearance. She knew from experience that
people who seemed to be bearing up well
under the weight of bad news might well
succumb to the shock later, and Miss
Blythe was no spring chicken. It was just
as well to give her proper treatment now.

Having removed some tablets from his
bag, Dr Dean turned Maudie. 'Give her
two of these immediately, Nurse. She
should nod off almost at once. Sit with
her until she wakes up again, and
telephone me if she shows any signs of
hysteria.' He left the room without
looking back. Bristling, Maudie did as she
was told. Left to herself, she would have
been happy to help the bereaved woman
in any way she could, but it would have
been nice to be asked!

'I'd better be getting back up there,'
Dick said. 'Will you be all right, Maudie?'

'Certainly.'

'I'll see you later, then.'

'And when you do, you can return my

cape!' said a sleepy voice from the bed. Maudie wondered whether that would be possible. Perhaps the cape would be impounded as evidence. They would have to wait and see.

★ ★ ★

During the hours that followed, Maudie had time to review the crime in her mind. There were missing pieces to this puzzle and the police would have to pursue many avenues to gather their evidence together. There was probably nothing that Maudie could do to help; yet she couldn't help thinking about it all.

Was Octavia the intended victim, or had she indeed been mistaken for her sister Myrtle? Who would want to do away with either of them, and why? Had Miss Blythe's accident at the river actually been attempted murder, as she kept asserting? It was all very well to dismiss the woman's talk of past lives as mere eccentricity, but what if there was some truth in what she was saying? Oh, not the fact that she might have had a previous existence, of course, but that somebody in this life was out to get her.

Maudie decided that whatever it was had nothing to do with Llandyfan. The answer must lie somewhere else. Where had Miss Blythe come from? Why was she staying here for no apparent reason? Where did her money come from? The woman could not be living on thin air.

Unfortunately these were queries that the police would have to make. Maudie could hardly ask such personal questions. With any luck, Dick might relay their findings to her before curiosity drove her mad.

'Curiosity killed the cat!' she reminded herself. Her brush with a killer the previous year had left her wary of putting herself in danger. Her favourite fictional sleuth, Miss Marple, would go about her investigations in a far more circumspect manner.

Of course, Octavia might have been the killer's target all along. Miss Blythe's belief that she had lived before might explain her notion that she was doomed now. Difficult husbands, death in child-birth, escape from battles and all the rest: all those 'memories' could prey on the mind.

Octavia now, that was different. She had been in America, hadn't she? What if she had been involved in something shady there, and had been followed back to England by somebody seeking revenge? An avid reader, Maudie knew something about the prohibition days, when liquor was officially banned in America but nevertheless imported and sold illegally. Rumrunners and the like were often shot dead by rival gangs or upholders of the law.

She sighed. As far as she knew, all that had happened back in the 1920s. Think again, Maudie! Well, the Americans had taken part in the recent world war, hadn't they? Suppose Octavia had learned something to the discredit of one of their servicemen? Someone who was a deserter, say? Or perhaps she had stumbled on a ring of black marketeers who consequently had been forced to silence her.

Fantasies, Maudie told herself. 'Really, Agatha Christie had better watch out! I'm sure I could write books like hers, if only I could find the time!' She stood up and walked around the room. Sitting on a hard wooden chair was no joke. She realized that she'd had nothing to eat since breakfast, and she was feeling decidedly grubby as well.

Responding to a tap on the door, she found Mrs Frost standing there with a tray in her hand. 'I'm on my way to bed, Nurse, but I thought you'd like a cup of tea,' she whispered.

'Greatly appreciated, I'm sure,' Maudie said. 'I was just thinking I might nip home and change my clothes, so if you hear the door opening and closing, you'll know what's up.'

'Do you really need to stay?' Mrs Frost said, eying the recumbent figure on the bed.

'I really don't think so. She's out for the count with those tablets Dr Dean gave her, and I've checked her vital signs several times, and all seems well. She's not ill, you know. She's just had a very nasty shock.'

'I tell you what, Nurse. There's a bed made up in the next room. I could sleep there, and I'd hear her if she wakes. I can always send for you if need be. I know you're on the phone, of course.'

Maudie considered this, and finally she nodded agreement. As long as somebody was within call, Miss Blythe hardly needed to be kept under observation. Dr Dean's abrupt order to Maudie could safely be ignored. It wasn't as if she was answerable to him at the moment, and in any case he hadn't said how long she was to remain, or whether someone would come to relieve her. Was she supposed to sit here like a bump on a log for the rest of the week? She swallowed her tea and handed the cup to Mrs Frost.

21

Rumours were flying round the district faster than bats flitting on a summer night.

'I hear they've found the owner of the knife what done her in,' the postman told Maudie, handing her a package that was too large to fit through the letterbox.

'Does that mean they know who the killer is, then?'

'Nah. It's one of them sheath knives what boy scouts like to mess around with. More for show than anything else if you ask me. Give me a good sharp penknife any time.'

'Oh, so the police are no further ahead, then?'

'I didn't say that, Nurse. The knife belongs to young Jimmy Barker, whose dad works up at the Bassett farm.'

'What on earth was he thinking of, leaving it lying around where anyone could pick it up?'

'I heard the youngsters were watching the doc judging that cake competition, drooling at the mouth, like. A nice slice was cut out of each cake for him to get a taste of; only, he just nibbled a little bit and left the rest. Thinking of his nice slim figure, no doubt.' Harry leered at Maudie. 'He's a handsome young feller. You could do worse than hang up your nurse's bonnet there, gal!'

'Handsome is as handsome does,' Maudie snapped.

'You don't think much of him, then?'

'I didn't say that, Harry.'

'You didn't have to. I can read that look in your eye. Anyway, Mrs Davis sees the kiddies watching and she takes pity on them and gives them a slice of Victoria jam sponge. Young Jimmy cuts it up to share with his mates and he sets the knife down while he scoffs his bit. When he goes to pick up the knife it's gone.'

'And nobody saw who took it?'

'Seems not. Well, I better get on. Can't have you keeping me here all day gossiping, Nurse.'

'Get along with you, Harry,' Maudie

said, laughing. 'So, bang goes my theory. If the killer was stalking Octavia Blythe — or Myrtle, as the case may be — the chap mustn't have come prepared to do the deed. He just picked up the knife and bumped her off on the spur of the moment.' She thought for a bit and revised her theory. Perhaps he had planned to strangle the woman but the knife had come to hand in time for him to use that instead. Or possibly he went to meet her in the tent on the pretext of having his fortune told. They quarrelled; he lost his temper, and struck the poor woman down.

Maudie wondered if she should pop round to ask Mrs Davis if she might have noticed someone picking up the knife. But no; surely the police would have asked her that already. Being all on edge to know if her cake would win the blue ribbon, she had probably kept a close watch on Dr Dean while he sampled the rest of the baking.

Would young Jimmy get his knife back after the case was solved? Perhaps it would be kept in some sort of black museum, accessible only to the police. She was quite sure that Mrs Barker would not give house room to the murder weapon but, knowing small boys as well as she did, she felt that Jimmy would probably delight in having such a souvenir.

Feeling in need of a pick-me-up, she went to make herself a cup of coffee, only to discover that her bottle of Camp essence was almost empty. She had meant to replace it but the murder had driven it out of her mind. Somehow she didn't fancy tea at that moment, and the weather was too warm for cocoa. Funny how tea and coffee didn't make you feel the same way.

Elbowing her way into the village shop past two small girls who were trying to decide between dolly mixtures and jelly babies, she found Helen Willis, reading the label on a bottle of HP Sauce as if her life depended on it. Her eyes were red-rimmed as if she might have hay fever, yet somehow Maudie suspected that the trouble was something more than that.

'Is everything all right, Mrs Willis? 'she whispered. 'Can I help at all?'

Helen jerked a finger towards the door. Correctly interpreting the gesture, Maudie followed her outside. Mrs Hatch, patiently listening to the little girls' debate, did not see them go.

'It's not a miscarriage, is it?' Maudie asked gently. She knew that the Willises were trying desperately for another child, only to have their hopes dashed with each month that went by.

'No, Nurse, but thanks for asking. No sign of anything yet, I'm afraid. It's Lily I'm worried about. I'm so afraid we're going to lose her.'

Those words, spoken to a nurse in another context, might mean that the child had some fatal illness, but Maudie knew what lay behind them.

'The mother is still determined to get Lily back, then.'

'We've had another letter. She says that some old friends are going out to Australia — emigrating, actually — and Lily can travel with them. She says they'll be getting in touch with us about the arrangements and we're supposed to take her to Southampton, or wherever it is they're sailing from, and hand her over to them there.'

'Oh, dear!'

'Can you imagine how she'll feel, Nurse, a child of that age? Handed over to complete strangers, spending weeks at sea with them on an old tub, probably getting sick as a dog, and crying for her mum? And that's me, Nurse! I may not have given birth to our Lily, but I'm the only mother she's ever know. At least, the only one she can remember.'

'I know.'

'And what's waiting for her at the end of it all? She'll be left with even more strangers. And that's what they are, Nurse! The man isn't even Lily's real father. He was killed at Dunkirk, you know. This chap is Ruth's second husband.'

'So what do you intend to do, Mrs Willis?'

'I've been to see a solicitor. And my, they know how to charge! He says we can raise a fuss and leave it to the courts to decide what's in the child's best interests, as he puts it.'

'And what does Lily have to say about all this?'

'I haven't dared say a word to her,' Mrs Willis said, mopping her eyes with a sodden handkerchief. 'But I'm sure she'll want to stay with us. It's the only home she's known, really.'

Maudie felt helpless. 'If there's anything I can do . . . ' she murmured, unable to think of a thing that would help the situation.

'Actually there is, Nurse. If we have to go to court, will you come and speak for us?'

'As a character witness, you mean, to give a report of you and your husband?'

'More to say how happy Lily is in our home. You've known her for a long time, Nurse. You helped our Polly when that bloke tried to steal her away.'

'Yes.' Maudie was thoughtful. 'I can do that. Just give me a bit of notice when the time comes and I'll make sure I'm free.'

★　★　★

'And that's where things stand at the moment,' Maudie told the vicar's wife. 'I've said I'll do what I can, but who is going to listen to me? I'm not a psychiatrist or a social worker.'

'Poor little soul. I expect she'll end up being handed over like a parcel. From what I've read in the papers, the courts usually side with the birth mother in these cases.'

'Maybe so, but where was this Ruth Martin all these years when she should have been in touch with Lily? Perhaps she didn't know that as far as Llandyfan was concerned, she was presumed dead in the blitz, but she seems to have used the death of the old grandmother as an excuse to disappear into a new life, one that didn't include her child. Of course the difficulty as far as the Willises are concerned is that they never tried to put their custody of Lily on a formal footing.'

'It makes me wonder how many other cases there are like this among the thousands of children who were evacuated during the war,' Mrs Blunt said sadly. 'Suppose, having sent their children to safety, parents were killed, either in the bombing or when they were serving in the armed forces. If there were no surviving relatives, what has become of the children? Have they all ended up in orphanages, or have some stayed on with their wartime hosts?'

'Don't ask me,' Maudie said, 'but I can tell you this. If I'm asked, I shall go to that court and do my very best for Lily Willis, and that's a promise!

22

Hearing footsteps, Maudie looked up from her filing and was delighted to see Dick Bryant approaching her office.

'Hello, Dick! What brings you here?'

'We've just heard that young Matt Flynn had recovered consciousness, and I've been sent to speak to him. Not that he can tell us much that we don't know already, but Sarge likes to get all the ends tied up whenever possible.'

'I'm glad to hear the boy's condition has improved. I wonder if he knows he's the father of a fine son?'

'Perhaps you'd like to break the news to him, if somebody hasn't already done it. I'm on my way to the hospital now, if you want to come along.'

Maudie jumped up with alacrity. 'That would be just the ticket. A patient of mine is in there. She had to go in for a caesarian section and I'd love to see her and the baby. I would have gone sooner, except it's a beast of a trip going to the cottage hospital by bus. Two changes and a long wait at the terminus in between.'

'Come on, then. Hop to it!' Dick said, turning to leave. Maudie snatched up her overcoat and followed him out, only pausing to lock the door on the way.

'Who is your patient, and why is she in hospital?' Dick asked, when they were speeding through the leafy lanes in the police car. 'Was there some terrible drama I'm not aware of?'

'It's Mrs Tolliver from Birch Lane,' Maudie told him. By now everyone in Llandyfan knew that the woman was in the cottage hospital, so she was not betraying patient confidentiality by relaying this information to Dick. 'She was sent there as a precautionary measure, that's all.'

'I see,' Dick said, accepting this without wanting to know more. Mrs. Tolliver was a slight woman with a small pelvis; and although she had successfully given birth to two children in the past, the babies grew bigger each time, and this latest addition was a burly ten pounder. Maudie

196

had judged that it might cause difficulties, and had recommended a caesarean section. It was always best to err on the side of caution.

'Is Matt being charged with anything?' she enquired now.

'Luckily for him, no. Under the circumstances his boss refuses to press charges, and he's even willing to take the boy back to work when he's fit. He says he doesn't want to kick a man when he's down.'

'That's decent of him.'

'Mind you, he may feel like changing his tune when he hears what the insurance company has to say. He's counting on getting something from the coverage he pays for on his garage property, but I very much doubt they'll approve that. Matt is an employee of the place and he took the vehicle without permission. I'm sure there are ramifications to that.'

'At least the three of them are alive. I shudder to think what might have happened to Greta if I hadn't been able to reach her in time. Dying in childbirth in the wreck of a stolen car is a fate I wouldn't wish on anyone.'

★ ★ ★

They found Matthew Flynn sitting up in bed, making a thorough nuisance of himself. 'I want to go home!' he roared, when Maudie and Dick entered the room.

'Things to do, places to go, I suppose,' Dick told him. 'Well, my lad, you are going to stay just where you are until the doctors say you can leave. Meanwhile, there are a few things I want to know.'

'I've got nothing to say, to you or anybody else,' the lad retorted, pouting. 'My head feels rotten. I feel like I've gone ten rounds with Joe Louis.'

Maude reflected that being knocked out by the heavyweight champion of the world could well have a similar effect to being rendered unconscious in a car accident. 'That's why you can't be discharged yet, Matt. There may have been some bruising of your brain and the doctors want you kept under observation for a while.'

'Huh!'

'Can you tell me what happened before the accident, Matt?' Dick had his notebook out and his fountain pen was poised for action.

Matt drew an arm across his head. 'It was raining, I think. We weren't going fast. Then something ran across in front of us — dark, like a shadow — and I had to slam on the brakes.'

'Greta tells us it was a loose horse.'

'Could have been. I can't remember. It all happened so fast.'

'And in which direction were you travelling?'

'I dunno. What do you mean?'

'Well, towards Llandyfan, or away from the village?'

'Oh, we were coming back, wasn't we? That was all down to Greta. First she says we have to go up to Scotland to get wed. Well, I thought it would be a bit of a lark, so I said I'd go along with it. We weren't ten miles down the road when she changes her mind. She says we have to get home right sharpish. Just like a woman that, always changing her mind. I was that fed up but she starts screeching, so I turned round at the next lay by and headed back. That's when it happened, I s'pose. All her fault, stupid wench.'

While she was aware that someone with a head injury might exhibit a change of personality afterwards, Maudie felt this was going too far. 'Greta acted sensibly once she realized the baby was on its way,' she told him. 'You do know you have a son, I suppose?'

'Nothing to do with me,' he muttered.

'Is that so? I hope you're not trying to deny you have a relationship with Greta, because I know differently.'

'Okay, so I had a thing going with her. That's only natural, innit? It don't mean I wanted a kid, or to settle down, neither!'

'They never do,' Maudie sighed, in answer to the look of disgust on Dick's face. 'Let's just hope this is the bump on the head talking.' She wouldn't have liked to be in Matt's shoes when Greta's father heard of this about-face. On one hand he might be pleased, considering the fact he'd been against the marriage all along. On the other hand he would certainly be furious at the insult to his daughter and would insist that the lad support his baby son, financially if not otherwise. Matt could find his income greatly reduced for years to come.

'I'll leave you to it,' Maudie told Dick. 'I must toddle along and see Mrs Tolliver before Matron starts her rounds.'

★ ★ ★

Maudie found Annie Tolliver sitting up in bed, looking pleased with herself. 'I'm leading the life of Riley!' she told Maude. 'It's grand, this is. Nine days lying in bed, waited on hand and foot, nothing to do but read magazines and eat chocs!'

'Everything all right at home, is it?'

'Bless you, yes! My sister has the little ones over at Midvale, and my mother-in-law is looking after my hubby. She was in yesterday, Mrs. Tolliver was. Ever so pleased it's a little boy this time. And they're all very kind in here, Nurse. Not that you weren't lovely to me when the other two came. It's just that this is a grand holiday for me, probably the only one I'll get this year. You know how it is, Nurse. If I'd done my lying-in at home I'd always be hopping up to see to something, so this is just grand.'

'Then mind you make the most of it. Do you have everything you need?'

'Oh, yes, I'm swimming in magazines and fruit. Sister is starting to get a bit fussy because my locker is overflowing with stuff. There's some magazines there that I've finished with, Nurse. How would you like to take one or two home with you to read? There's some good articles in this one here.' She waved a colourful magazine under Maudie's nose.

'I don't mind if I do, unless you'd like to share them with one of the other women on the ward?

'Oh, they get plenty of choice when the lady comes round with the book trolley. She has some good hospital romances on that. I've been through two of them already. Lovely, they are. Have you ever thought of finding a handsome doctor for yourself, Nurse?'

'Not lately,' Maudie said grimly, with Dr Dean in mind.

23

'Would you mind hanging on for a bit?' Dick asked when they met in the vestibule. 'A chap I know from next door is in here after having his appendix out. I'd like to pop in for a few moments to say hello.'

'Don't get caught by Matron, then,' Maudie warned. 'This isn't visiting hours, you know. We were only let in this morning because I'm checking on my patient and you were here on official business. But no, I shan't mind waiting. I'll have a stroll round the grounds. The flower beds are rather nice here.'

Rounding a corner past a small fountain, she came upon a woman of her own age sitting on a wooden bench, throwing crumbs to the birds. 'Hello. You're the night sister here, aren't you?'

The woman looked up. 'Oh, hello, Nurse. Here to see another patient, are you? I know we've discharged your young girl and her little boy.'

'Mrs Tolliver. She's one of mine.'

'Oh, yes. She had the section, and is doing very well.'

'Do you mind if I sit down?' Maudie asked. 'I'm waiting for my lift back to Llandyfan and there's something I'd like to ask you.'

'Certainly. What did you want to know?'

'The last time I was here I mentioned a new doctor we have in our district, a Donald Dean, and you didn't seem to care much for him.'

'I'm sorry. I shouldn't let my personal feelings show.'

'I have a reason for asking. You see, my job is being threatened by this man and, well, I'd feel happier if I knew if he was known for being difficult. I love my work and I don't want to move, but I really feel he intends to drive me out.'

The sister was silent for a moment, and then she lifted her eyes to gaze at Maudie. 'Very well, I'll tell you, for all the help it may be. Before coming here I worked in a hospital in Surrey, where I was the sister on a men's surgical ward. Dean was on the staff there. We found him to be a very arrogant man, but you know that already.'

'Go on.'

'One of my staff nurses was new there and she made the mistake of giving a hug to a patient who had just received word that his wife had died. It was not the sort of thing we encourage, as you well know, Nurse, but under the circumstances I really couldn't blame her. Unfortunately Dr Dean happened to come in at the wrong moment, saw what was happening and proceeded to dress her down in front of everybody: probationers, patients, the lot. He accused her of unprofessional conduct, saying that he would report her to Matron and get her dismissed.'

'Ouch!'

'I suggested to him that I should be allowed to administer discipline on my own ward, whereupon he compounded the problem by saying that as I obviously couldn't control my staff I wasn't fit to be in charge. The poor girl was devastated, and you can imagine how I felt. I went to Matron myself of course, thinking it wise to get in first, but as it turned out Dr Dean is Matron's nephew, so she was less than sympathetic.'

'Oh, dear!'

'The upshot was that I decided to move on; not altogether because of that episode, mind you, so now I work here.'

'And what about the nurse? Surely she wasn't dismissed?'

'Oh, no, but each time Dr Dean did rounds in the ward he either ignored the girl completely or made disparaging remarks, and in the end it all became too much for her. She gave in her notice and she works in a flower shop now. What a waste of a good nurse!'

'I could murder that man!' Maudie said fiercely.

'Yes, well don't let him do the same to you. Now if that's all you want to know, I must get home. It was a long night, and my bed is waiting for me.'

Maudie watched her go. What if the man turned up at one of her deliveries and criticized her in her patient's hearing? She would brain him with the bedpan! She couldn't really, of course, and there lay the difficulty. Most of the time it was the doctor who held the winning cards.

'There you are! All ready to go home?' If only all men could be more like Dick. Maudie smiled at him and followed him to the car.

★ ★ ★

'You can let me out here,' Maudie said, when they neared the Blacks' home. 'I want to give Greta the news about Matt, if she hasn't heard already.'

'Right ho. How will you get home?'

'Shank's pony. It's a lovely day. I may as well make the most of it.'

'He's come to, then, young Matt,' Mrs Black said at the door.

'Oh, you've heard, then.'

'Sally Tolliver dropped in. She'd been to see their Annie and the new little one. She heard the news up at the hospital and went to the men's ward to see for herself.'

'Does Greta know, then? And Mr Black?'

'My hubby was that furious I thought he'd have an apoplexy! Almost foaming at the mouth, he was, when the old bat told us what the boy was supposed to have said.'

'Which was?'

'Oh, that he never wanted to wed our Greta. It was her who talked him into it. That sort of rot. Wanting to weasel out of his responsibility now that little Frankie is actually here and not just an idea.'

'I thought that Mr Black was against the marriage. Wasn't that what sent them haring off to Gretna Green in the first place?'

'He didn't want them to get wed, Nurse; of course he didn't. Seventeen and nineteen, that's too young. But young Matt taking advantage, and then jilting the girl before the whole parish, that's another thing entirely.'

'Yes, I can see that. But I have to ask this, Mrs Black. What happens to young Frankie now?'

'Oh, Frank has come round to letting us keep the child. After all, he's our own flesh and blood. But how we're to bear the disgrace I don't know. First that boy gets her into trouble, and now he makes out she isn't good enough to wed. If I could get my hands on him I'd wring his neck, Nurse, I would really!'

'Come now, Mrs Black. Surely you don't think he's worth swinging for? Your job now is to make sure your husband doesn't do anything silly. Now then, shall I have a look at Greta and the baby?'

She found Greta in her room, idly leafing through the ever-present film magazines. The baby lay in his treasure cot beside her, waving his little legs in the air and blowing bubbles. The girl refused to meet Maudie's eyes.

'I suppose you've heard, then? Matt's decided to wake up?' Greta said.

'Yes, I've just been to the hospital as a matter of fact.'

'Well, he can rot there, for all I care!'

'I know that what he's saying at the moment is painful for you to hear, Greta, but he may change his tune when he's more fully recovered. Head injuries can be difficult things; they seldom heal overnight.'

'So what! Dad was right all along, see.

209

He keeps telling me nineteen isn't a man, it's just a lad with foolish ideas. Wed in haste, repent at leisure, that's what Dad says. And he's right, too. I'm well out of it, that's what I am!'

'I shouldn't be too quick to judge, dear,' Maudie murmured. 'You think that way now because you're hurt and scared, but when young Matt comes calling with a posy in his hand, your troubles will melt away like snow in the sunshine.'

'Phooey!' snapped Greta. She picked up her magazine and began to study it pointedly. 'See this? It's a picture of Gregory Peck. Isn't he lovely? Why aren't there any men like him around Llandyfan? You tell me that, Nurse!'

Maudie stared sadly at the girl, who had not yet learned the difference between real life and fantasy. Gregory Peck was a lovely man on the silver screen, but that was just an illusion. Who knew what he might be like when the studio lights were dimmed and he had gone home to his Hollywood mansion? It was a conundrum.

'I'll be on my way, then,' she said. 'I'll

look in on you another day.' There was no answer. The baby gurgled in an appealing fashion, ignored by his young mother. Maudie sighed and left the room.

24

Dressed in a cotton nightgown with scuffed slippers on her feet, Maudie was lying on her bed with the windows wide open to let in the breeze. She had Annie's magazines to leaf through, and very interesting they looked, too. She studied the table of contents in the first one.

'Keeping the Mystery in Your Marriage'. That looked interesting. Marriage itself was a mystery to her, but she saw a great deal of other people's marriages from the inside. Her patients often confided in her, asking her advice about relationship problems in the belief that nurses, and midwives in particular, had specialist knowledge about life. This article might provide useful information. She turned to the appropriate page.

She discovered that you were supposed to digest the advice, given by a well-known agony aunt, and then rate yourself according to your current behaviour. At the end of the article you would either give yourself a pat on the back or see where there was room for improvement. Interested, Maudie looked at the first section. 'Do you wear curlers to bed?' the writer demanded. Apparently doing so could spell the death of a marriage, or desire, at least. That explained why so many local women could be seen out and about by day with curlers protruding from beneath their workaday turbans. They were beautifying themselves after their husbands left for work.

Maudie was able to give herself a point for that. With her long, glossy hair worn in a bun, or an elegant chignon on the rare occasions she went out to some fancy social event, she had no need of curlers. This was easy! She was well in control of the mystery surrounding her person, and she wasn't even married!

Section two had to do with makeup. You were supposed to spare your husband the distress of seeing you bare-faced and bleary-eyed in the morning. You could avoid this by getting up half an hour early and 'putting your face on' before your man woke up. Maudie could see it now: some sleep-deprived mother slathering make-up on while her husband slept.

She herself made do with a dab of powder on her nose and a smear of lipstick, hurriedly applied before she rushed out of the door in the morning. Her main aid to beauty was Pond's Cold Cream. It wasn't that she was slapdash. In her training, hospital nurses had been forbidden to use cosmetics, and for all she knew the rule might apply across the profession. No points for section two!

'Never leave your unmentionables draped across the radiator to dry,' Auntie cautioned. 'This is a sight that will not endear you to your husband, who expects you to keep an orderly home.' Maudie's cottage didn't possess radiators. Any heat there was came from an open fire. On wet days she hung her smalls in the scullery to let them drip dry. Did that count as slatternly behaviour? She was afraid that it did. She had noticed the sneer on Dr Dean's face when he had made that unexpected tour of her home.

After a day spent scrubbing and polishing, housewives were supposed to change their clothes and pretty themselves up in readiness to welcome their husbands home. They never slopped around half-dressed, as Maudie was doing now! Nevertheless, she awarded herself anther point because she always dressed attractively when Dick came over to spend the evening with her.

At the end of the exercise she had a score of two out of ten, which reminded her of her old school reports that usually bore the words 'Can do better'. With a grunt of exasperation, she hurled the magazine across the room. She was a contented single woman, so why should she bother about keeping the mystery in a non-existent marriage?

The sort of mystery that appealed to her was the one that was hanging over Llandyfan right now. Like everybody else, she wanted to know who had killed Octavia. She was sure that Myrtle Blythe held the key. Why not go and have a word with her? Maudie sprang out of bed, ready for action. It was her day off, but what was wrong with going to the inn to make a neighbourly call on the bereaved woman?

★　★　★

'Oh, it's you again!' Miss Blythe snapped when she opened the door to Maudie. 'Can't you people leave me alone?'

'I'm your nurse,' Maudie said, stretching a point. 'I needed to make sure that you're all right. I know that you must be so shocked and upset about the death of your sister.'

'You know nothing of the sort! If you must know, I hated Octavia and I'm not sorry she's dead!'

'Oh, dear!' Maudie was taken aback for a moment. Rallying, she found the excuse she needed. 'May I come in for a moment, Miss Blythe? You see, I have to make a report on your condition to Dr Dean. I'd like to take your blood pressure and so on, just to be on the safe side.'

'Very well, you may come in, but you mustn't keep me long.' Maudie consoled herself with the thought that it wasn't a total falsehood. It was quite possible that the doctor would ask about Miss Blythe, and it was as well to be prepared where that man was concerned.

'I'm sorry to hear there was bad blood between you and your sister,' she murmured, when she was returning the sphygmomanometer to her bag. 'Would you like to tell me why that was?'

'How impertinent you are, Nurse! I don't know when I've met such a nosy parker! I suppose it comes from the coarseness of your trade. Always dealing with the more brutal side of life.'

'It's been my experience that negative thoughts weigh heavily on the mind, Miss Blythe. Confession is good for the soul, they say.'

'Confession! Are you accusing me of having murdered Octavia? My own sister!'

'I used the word in the sense of unburdening yourself, Miss Blythe.' But it could have happened on the spur of the moment, Maudie thought to herself. She could have come across the knife, put down for a moment by the young Boy

Scout, and taken it to the fortune teller's tent. Naturally her sister would have suspected nothing when she saw who it was. Miss Blythe would then have moved round to her back, plunged in the knife, and left the tent. Yes, it could have happened that way. And, perfect lady that she was, she always went out wearing gloves, didn't she, so that would dispose of any danger of fingerprints on the murder weapon.

'Oh, very well! You may as well know the whole story. I'm afraid it's bound to come out in the end, either through this place or those nasty newspaper reporters.'

'May I sit down?'

'Please yourself. This won't take long.' Miss Blythe arranged herself on the one chair in the room, leaving Maudie standing. Having no wish to loom over the woman, fearing that a threatening aspect that might stem the flow of her words, Maudie perched on the bed. This was a measure of her eagerness to hear what Miss Blythe had to say. For a nurse, sitting on a bed was a sin of the worst order. Nurses had been sent to Matron for less.

'Yes?' she prompted. 'Had your sister done something to upset you?'

'She stole my husband, Nurse. Can any woman do worse to a sister?'

'Your husband? But you're not married, Miss Blythe.'

'Very well; my fiancé, then.'

'But surely that must have been years ago?'

'Of course it was. I recall it quite clearly. 1805. Admiral Lord Nelson had just won the battle of Trafalgar.'

'Oh, I see.' Disappointment hit Maudie like a slap in the face. The woman was back in the past, rambling on about one of her past lives. 'That has nothing to do with the twentieth century, then, has it? Couldn't you forgive her for something that happened more than a century ago?' And why are we having this mad conversation? she added silently.

'Not when she followed me into this life, Nurse! She only came to gloat. I'm sure of that.'

'I don't quite understand.'

'Octavia was my half-sister, Nurse. My mother died when I was quite young, but I did my utmost to be a consolation to my father. He allowed me to direct the servants and I took delight in ordering his favourite meals for him, and seeing that his garments were kept in good repair.'

Maudie thought she could see what was coming next. Papa had found someone new and married her, and naturally the new wife had taken over the running of the household. Little Myrtle's nose had been put out of joint. Probably Papa had believed he was doing the right thing by letting his daughter revert to child-status, relieved of adult cares. When baby sister put in an appearance it was the last straw.

'All her life Octavia has been petted and pampered,' Miss Blythe said, confirming Maudie's diagnosis. 'Everything I had, she wanted; and if I wouldn't give it to her she howled until the grownups came and made me hand it over. 'Poor little Occy. You're a big girl, Myrtle. Why won't you share your dolly with her little sister?''

Maudie nodded. In her job she had seen this sort of thing time and time again. The toddler of the family, who up until the arrival of the next baby had been the centre of attention, was almost ignored while its harrassed mother tried to cope with the new demands placed upon her. Sleepless nights and not enough hours in the day to do everything she had to accomplish could make the best of mothers fall short in the affection department. More than once she had caught an angry toddler in the act of trying to poke a new sibling in the eye, and how could you reason with an innocent two-year-old? It was hard to make him understand.

'So what did you do about it, Miss Blythe?'

'Do? What could I do? I just had to put up with it as best I could. I had the last laugh, though!'

'Oh, yes?'

'I've got the money, you see. She wanted it, but she couldn't have it. It was as simple as that.'

Maudie frowned. 'I don't quite understand.'

'My mother came from a wealthy
family, Nurse. When my grandfather died
he left me a sizeable inheritance. As I told
you, Octavia was my half-sister. Grand-
papa left her nothing. Why should he?
And I must say I find this talk of money
quite distasteful, Nurse. A lady never
discusses such matters, but perhaps you
wouldn't know that.'

'I didn't mean to pry,' Maudie fibbed.

'I certainly don't know what else one
would call it,' Miss Blythe snapped. 'Now,
if you don't mind I'll ask you to go. I
need to lie down.'

'Do send for me if I can be of
assistance at any time,' Maudie said
sweetly, closing the door behind her.

25

'Have you seen The *Chronicle*, Nurse?'
Mrs Hatch pointed to the pile of
newspapers on the counter. 'There's ever
such an interesting piece about the
murder, written by that young chap who
was here on the day of the fête. According
to him, they think the husband did it.'

'Whose husband?'

'Why, that Madam Zora, of course.'

'But she was a maiden lady, surely?'

'That's not what that reporter says.
Here, take a look at this, Nurse. I just
can't get over it!'

'I'll take a paper with me and read it
later,' Maudie said, handing over the
money. She walked back to her cottage,
quite forgetting that she had gone to the
shop to buy cream of tartar, and had left
without it.

She was thoroughly confused by all this
talk of husbands. If she went on like this
she'd end up with her wits as scattered as

those of Myrtle Blythe. Back at home she put the kettle on and while she waited for it to boil she unfolded the *Chronicle*, hoping for edification.

The story was on the front page, which was no surprise considering the lack of hard news that usually characterized what its readers usually referred to as 'the local rag'. A headline reading '*Killer At Large in Village*' was blazoned across the front page in black lettering. The size of the type was a bit much, but perhaps the story warranted it. At any rate, it beat hands down any talk of 'Keeping the Mystery in Your Marriage', Maudie decided.

The kettle began to whistle, making her jump. When she was settled with a pot of strong tea and a ginger nut, she paid more attention to the article, which she dismissed as a lot of rot. Murder stalking the church fête, mysterious killer at the cake competition, psychic killed by mistake.

What a load of tripe! The only item of interest was a statement that Madam Zora was actually the wife of an American businessman, Wilbur Brownlow. The gentleman in question was reported to be 'devastated by the death of his lovely wife'. How had the reporter got hold of this information if the police had not? Or had he actually obtained this piece of news from them? And if so, why hadn't Dick Bryant put her in the picture rather than leaving her to find out about it second-hand? And another thing . . . Why hadn't Myrtle Blythe explained that Octavia was a married woman? Or had she? Was Brownlow the man that she had accused her sister of stealing from her? Given the woman's state of mind, it was all too easy to dismiss her ramblings as so much nonsense — but did they perhaps contain a grain of truth? Once again, Maudie's mind veered around to the possibility that Myrtle might have killed her sister.

* * *

Maudie and Dick came out of the Odeon feeling satisfied with their evening's entertainment. Having seen *Road to Rio*, they had enjoyed the antics of Bob Hope and Bing Crosby and were hoping that more films in the comedy series would be made as time went on.

'Although it's that Dorothy Lamour you really go for,' Maudie teased her friend.

'A cat may look at a king,' Dick quoted.

'Except that kings don't wear sarongs!'

'I suppose you'll want to go to that Moira Shearer film we saw on the trailer,' Dick grumbled, having been unimpressed by their preview of *The Red Shoes*. 'Ballet is not my style, I'm afraid. All that hopping about in tights; it seems an odd way of going on to me.'

'Well, I'd like to see it but I won't force you to go. Perhaps Mrs Blunt can be persuaded. She hardly ever gets a day off from parish duties and I'm sure she'd enjoy a drama that doesn't involve quarrel in the Mothers' Union!'

They had reached the chip shop now, and Maudie rushed to bag a corner table while Dick ordered two helpings of plaice and chips and three penn'orth of crispy bits. Maudie gave a sigh of pleasure as the first vinegar-soaked chip reached her taste buds.

'I've got a bone to pick with you, Dick Bryant,' she announced when she had downed her fish and most of her chips.

'Oh, yes? What's that about, then?'

'I suppose you've seen The *Chronicle?*

'Yes, well?'

'You didn't tell me that Madam Zora has a husband.'

'Oh, that.' Dick licked his fingers after swallowing the last of his crispy bits.

'I do think you're mean. You might have said something. I thought we were supposed to be friends.'

He looked at her sternly. 'In the first place, this is police business, Maudie. There are some things we don't make public until the time is right.'

'Pooh! It couldn't have been any big secret if they told that reporter.'

'Actually, we gave him nothing at all. The inspector was furious when he saw that article, going on about that chap withholding evidence.'

'Go on. Then how did he find out about this Wilbur whatsit chap?'

'He says he had it from Myrtle Blythe.'

'What! But I've just been to see her and she didn't tell me! Although wait a minute. She did say that Zora — Octavia, that is — had stolen her fiancé from her.'

'And you didn't see fit to pass that little nugget on to the police?'

'No, because I believed she was wittering on about something that happened in a past life. Old Wilbur's name was never mentioned. Besides, I understand that your detective chaps went to interview the old girl right after the murder happened. Why didn't they wring it out of her then?'

Dick shrugged. Possibly Maudie wasn't the only one who had written off the old dear as a bit barmy.

'I think she did it,' Maudie remarked. 'She had the motive. She loathed her sister — half-sister, that is — who by all accounts was a thorn in her side all her life. And why did old Zora come back to England at all, if she had a life and a perfectly good husband in America?'

'Ah, but was he a perfectly good husband, as you put it? If he's such a hero, why didn't he come forward when his wife was killed? This is not an official statement, but just between us, my money is on him.'

'Let me finish, will you? Octavia always envied Myrtle, and wanted her share of whatever big sister had. Myrtle has money, pots of it to hear her talk, inherited from her grandpa. Octavia, being the child of Dad Blythe's second marriage, got nothing. Suppose she came back to England for the express purpose of winkling some of the cash out of Myrtle. Myrtle has had enough of this, and when the scout knife comes to hand she goes and finishes Madam Zora off.'

'That's all very neat, Maudie, but as I said, we're taking a close look at the husband now. He hasn't come forward to claim his wife's body, but he must be in England if that reporter has spoken to him.'

'Then ask the reporter where the man is.'

'Easier said than done, I'm afraid. He keeps waffling on about journalistic integrity and the need to protect his sources. To hear him talk, anyone would think he'd signed the Official Secrets Act. Unfortunately we're not allowed to bring out the thumbscrews nowadays.'

'So what's your theory, Dick?'

'Off the record, it goes something like this. The couple come over from America, hoping to get money out of Myrtle Blythe. For some reason the husband decides he wants to rid himself of Octavia, so he kills her.'

'Then why wait to do it at the church fête? Why not push her over the rail when they're on board ship? Tragic accident: British ex-pat plunges to her death in mid-Atlantic.'

'A spur-of-the-moment decision?'

'Yes, but when he went to the tent, why would his wife just sit there, meekly waiting to be killed?'

'Yes, but that's why she *would* sit still, you see. She'd have no reason to suspect her own husband.'

'Somebody must have seen something,' Maudie muttered. 'I suppose the killer came and went though the door of the tent and didn't crawl in the back way?'

'Not only that, but the toggles were fastened on the outside and somebody had hung a 'Closed' sign on the tent. Those two girls who found the body swear blind that's how they found it. There was so much coming and going, what with the band playing and everyone shouting during the tug of war and the kiddies' races.'

'Will your lot ever get to the bottom of this, Dick?'

He pulled a face. 'If we don't, you can always read all about it in The *Chronicle!* It seems to me that young reporter has a fertile imagination!'

26

Gracie Fields was belting out a song on the wireless as Maudie skipped around her living room, flicking a duster here and there. It was a bright morning and she felt like singing along with the famous singer.

'Let him go, let him tarry, let him sink or let him swim; he doesn't care for me and I don't care for him . . . '

A hesitant rapping at the door came as an unwelcome interruption. Taking a hasty peep at herself in the hall mirror, Maudie went to answer the door. She just hoped it wasn't that Dr Dean again, coming to establish his claim to her home. 'Like a tom cat spraying on the furniture,' she grumbled under her breath.

The woman waiting on the doorstep was short, skinny and wore an anxious expression. Frizzy hair topped a face that had too many frown lines for her age.

'Yes? Can I help you?'

'Nurse Rouse? The midwife?'

'Yes, that's me.'

'I'm sorry to bother you at home, Nurse, but I couldn't wait for office hours. I have to get to work, you see.'

'Oh, yes?' Would the woman ever come to the point? She seemed too long in the tooth to want to register for a home birth; perhaps she wanted advice on the problems of menopause.

'I'm Angie Flynn. I'd really like to talk to you.'

Light dawned. 'You must be Matt's mother. Do come in.'

Maudie ushered the woman into the kitchen, where she dithered around for a moment before accepting a chair. Maudie did not offer tea. She had already rinsed the teapot and now she was running late. It was best to get this over with as quickly as possible.

'I want you to have a word with that Greta, Nurse. She's trying to keep my grandson from me and I have a right to see him, don't I?'

'Do I gather that the marriage is off, then? Greta and Matt have broken off their engagement, have they? I suppose it's her father. He's been against it from the beginning.'

'Oh, that's not just Frank. It's my Mickey as well. He doesn't want to see the lad tied down at nineteen. And supposing they did get married: how would they live? The pair of them would have to move in with us, or else settle in at the Blacks' place. No, I'd just as soon not have that.'

'And?' Maudie prompted.

'Well, it's like this. Young Greta went to see Matt in the hospital and when she got there she found all his mates round the bed, laughing and joking. She ran out of there in a snit, shouting how she never wanted to see him again, plus a few choice words I wouldn't care to repeat!'

'That seems a bit drastic.'

'Yes, well, that Linda Bates was there too, lolling on the bed and daring Greta to say anything about it. Of course, that was like a red rag to a bull, as you can imagine.'

'Linda Bates. I don't think I know her.'

'Oh, she's a brazen little piece, all of

fifteen. She works at the dairy in Brookfield. The thing is, she's had her sights set on our Matt ever since they were at school together and it seems she's determined to get her hooks into him now.'

'And how does Matt feel about that?'

'He's flattered, of course. The trouble is, his mates think he's the big man now, him being a father and all, and it's given him a high opinion of himself.'

'Well, Mrs Flynn, your Matt *is* a father now and he has responsibilities,' Maudie said sternly. 'It seems to me that poor Greta has a right to be upset if he's thrown her over. She'll have to spend the next twenty years or so bringing up his child, while he gets off light-hearted and fancy free!'

'That's just what she said. 'You needn't think you're having anything to do with your boy if you abandon us now, Matt Flynn.' That's what she told him! But baby Frankie is my only grandchild, Nurse, and I need to be part of his life. You know these people. I want you to talk to them. Appeal to Greta's mother. Tell them I'll have my rights!'

'I don't know that I should interfere, Mrs Flynn. Might it not be better for your husband to have a word with Frank Black, man to man? I take it that Matt means to support Frankie financially? Perhaps when the Blacks see that he's doing all he can they may change their minds and give him access to the child.'

'Oh, he'll be doing that all right! That Frank went to see Matt's boss and told him to knock a few bob off his wages each week, to be paid over straight to Frank. The cheek of it!'

Maudie looked at the clock on the wall. She hoped that nobody was waiting outside her office door. It would be just her luck for Dr Dean to roll in on the one day when she was late opening up. Still, this was official business in a way.

'That's one way of doing things, I suppose, and you can hardly blame Mr Black. Let's face it; he'll have to support Greta and the baby for some time to come. She won't be able to get a job now, with a new baby to care for.'

'It's hard on the boy, though,' his

mother grumbled. 'By the time he pays that, and gives me something for his keep, there won't be much left for anything else. That little hussy Linda won't last long if he can't take her to the pictures or out dancing.'

'Pity!'

'Yes, well, I've said my piece and I'd better be going before I get my own wages docked. Please think about what I've said, Nurse. I'd be ever so grateful.'

'I will say something if I get the chance, Mrs Flynn, but no promises, mind.'

Closing the door behind her visitor, Maudie was moved to feel sorry for the woman. What must it be like to have an unsatisfactory son, and a grandchild that one wasn't allowed to see? Life could be hard, and this muddle was not of Angie Flynn's making.

As she buttoned herself into her uniform dress, Maudie began to sing again, the cheerful tune that Gracie Fields had made popular. 'He can go and get another, that I hope he will enjoy, for I'm going to marry a far nicer boy!'

That should be Greta Black's signature

tune. Maudie devoutly hoped that the girl would recover from her heartache in time and that her baby would grow up to be a credit to her. She was lucky in that after their original distress and indignation her parents were standing by her; all too often pregnant girls were shown the door by outraged parents and never welcomed back into the family circle.

* * *

As she had feared, someone was waiting for Maudie in the parish hall. Helen Willis was pacing up and down, pausing every now and then to dab at her swollen eyes with the comer of her headscarf.

'I'm so sorry to keep you waiting, Mrs Willis. Someone came to see me at the house and I couldn't get away earlier,' Maudie explained, unlocking her office door as she spoke. 'Do come in and sit down.'

'That's all right, Nurse. I shouldn't have come, really, but I felt if I didn't talk to someone I'd burst!'

'It's Lily, I suppose.'

'We've had a summons to go to court. You'll be getting one as well, I expect. And what's worse, they sent someone from the social to talk to the child, and now she's all upset.'

'I'm sorry to hear she's upset, but it might be a good sign that the authorities are willing to listen to Lily's feelings on the situation. Did she venture an opinion at all?'

'She can't stop crying. All she can say is, 'I don't want that other Mummy. I want Mummy Helen and Uncle Bob.' That's what she calls my hubby, Nurse. For some reason she's never called him Dad.'

'Please try not to worry,' Maudie said. 'I'm sure that everything will turn out for the best.'

'Are you, Nurse? I wish I had your confidence.'

Maudie patted the distraught woman on the arm. More and more she seemed to be taking on the role of family counsellor. Maybe she should hang out her shingle!

27

'Was there something else, Mrs Willis?' Maudie sensed that her visitor was reluctant to leave.

'You know how it said on the wireless that the police want to talk to anyone who went to see Madam Zora the day she was killed?'

'Yes. I believe they're trying to establish the time of death.'

'I was there, Nurse.'

'And have you told this to the police?'

'That's it, you see. I felt that silly, and I didn't want Bob to know I wasted good money going to see a fortune-teller.'

'Oh, it's just a bit of fun,' Maudie assured her. 'Nobody really believes in that sort of thing, but it's all cash in hand for the church fête. Not that the poor woman had time to tell many fortunes, I suppose. It's too bad she couldn't foretell what was in her own future, or she might still be alive.'

'I was hoping she could tell me what's going to happen to our Lily. You must think I'm that stupid.'

Maudie said nothing. She had been in nursing long enough to know that in times of trouble we find our comfort where we can. Who was she to judge how a grieving mother should behave?

'And now I'm afraid to go to the police,' Helen went on, 'because they'll say I should have come sooner. What am I going to do, Nurse?'

'You'll have to say something, of course, but perhaps I can help. I know Dick Bryant. If you like I could pass on a message from you, and if the detectives wish to speak to you, they can get in touch.'

'Oh, would you, Nurse? I'd be ever so grateful!'

'So tell me more. What time did you get there?'

'At Madam Zora's tent? I'm not sure, because my watch stopped. It was just after the band struck up, though. 'Land of Hope and Glory', that's what they were playing.'

'That's good. Now, were you her first customer, do you think?'

'No, I wasn't. A chap came out just when I was passing by the hoopla stall.'

Maudie tried to hide her excitement. 'Did you get a good look at him?'

'I suppose I stared a bit. It seemed odd, a man his age going to consult a fortune-teller. I mean, blokes don't much go for that sort of thing, do they? It's all cars and football with them.'

'He wasn't young, then. Not the sort of fellow who'd want to know if he had a chance with the girl he fancied. Tall, short? Fat, thin?'

'Taller than me, with a fat stomach on him, like his chest had slipped down over his belt, if you know what I mean.'

Maudie did. 'And what was this man wearing? Did you notice that?'

'He was dressed a bit funny. Not like the chaps round these parts. He had on a suit in a sort of cream colour, and a soft sort of hat. Oh, and his shoes were funny, too. Partly brown and partly white.'

'Did he have a tie at all?'

'Not what I'd call a tie. A thing like bits

of cord hanging round his neck.'

He sounds American, Maudie thought. She had seen enough Hollywood films to recognize the type. No Englishman would dress in such a fashion, even if such garments could be found in Britain. Could this be the mysterious Mr Wilbur Brownlow?

'You're very observant, Mrs Willis. I'm sure the police will be pleased to hear from you. Now, one last question: was Madam Zora alive when you saw her?'

Helen blinked. 'Oh, yes. She read the cards for me, but it was no good. In the end I wished I hadn't gone. She kept on about a journey across the water, and what could that mean but poor little Lily sent off to Australia?' Tears welled up in her eyes again and Maudie stood up hastily, hoping to forestall another dose of the waterworks.

'I shall inform Dick at once,' she said, smiling. 'You can count on me.'

Snivelling, Helen Willis turned to leave.

*　*　*

Lunchtime couldn't come fast enough for Maudie. All this drama had given her an appetite. She had spoken to Dick on the phone and he had promised to pass the information on. Now she had nothing pressing to do until mid-afternoon, so she could devote herself to a leisurely meal. Should she go to the Copper Kettle and order a bowl of their homemade soup, or should she go home and boil an egg? The egg won.

The postman had called in her absence and she discovered several letters lying on the doormat. 'Bills, by the look of it,' she groaned. Sure enough, she was requested to fork over far too much of her modest salary to appease the gas company and the electricity board. She ripped open an official-looking missive, giving herself a paper cut in the process.

Sucking her finger, she read that she was asked to attend a court hearing in front of the magistrates to decide the case of 'the minor child Lily Martin, known as Willis'. Well, she was glad to have the chance to do something to help the family. If only she knew what she'd be asked to say.

Her heart gave an unpleasant thump when she turned to the remaining letter. It bore the logo of the local council in one corner, and it could mean only one thing. This small envelope contained her fate. Her whole future would be decided in a few short lines of typewritten material. She didn't need a clairvoyant to tell her that the news was probably bad.

She slit the thing open and then found that she didn't have the strength to take out the letter. She threw the horrid thing down on the table and lowered herself into an armchair, looking around the familiar room as if in pain. She loved this old cottage, with its uneven walls, its low ceilings and its latticed windows. Generations of villagers had lived here through good times and bad, and none more happily than Nurse Maudie Rouse. How could she bear to leave it? And more than that, how could she bear to think of Dr Dean living here in her place?

Would he tend the climbing rose at the front door as lovingly as Maudie had done? She had fed it and cared for it until it was the pride of the neighbourhood. The beastly man would probably rip it out and cast the pretty thing on the bonfire!

She glanced at the letter again. What was the point of putting off the evil moment? It would only nag at her all day if she didn't know the worst now.

The letter was short and sweet. It informed her that in view of the fact that the provisions of the National Health Act had not come into play until July of this year, 1948, council had decided that her contract with them should be extended for another year. At the end of that time the situation would be reviewed. They were hers sincerely, *et cetera*.

Maudie ran into the kitchen and vomited into the sink. Reprieve! Of course it made sense that it would take time to implement the new way of doing things. Surely more personnel would have to be hired and duties reassigned, now that people could seek treatment free of charge. And there would always be a place for midwives in the new order, for babies would keep arriving, world without end!

What about her home, though? Turning on the tap to rinse the sink, Maudie felt the spirit of wartime Britain rising in her breast. This was a tied cottage, one that went with her job. She paid her rent. Why should Dr Johnny-come-lately push her out? He owned a car, didn't he? Let him find a place in Brookfield or Midvale.

She curled her fist into a defiant salute, remembering Britain's wartime hero, Winston Churchill.

'Good old Winnie! she shouted. 'We shall fight them in the streets! We shall never surrender!'

She needed to share her good news with somebody. Her friend Joan Blunt would do. Mrs Davis, coming out of her house to take the dog for a walk, was later to report that she had seen Nurse Rouse tearing down the road with her hair tumbling down and no hat on.

'There must have been a real emergency,' she told her husband that night. 'Another accident, say, or some woman's labour gone wrong.'

'You must've got it wrong, old girl,' he told her.' I didn't hear about anything like that at the pub.'

But Mrs Davis was an avid reader of hospital romances, and she knew that a nurse is never allowed to run except in cases of fire or haemorrhage, and she knew what she had seen.

28

Maudie duly reported to the court at Midvale. Her hands felt damp as she waited to be called on. Three stern magistrates were seated on a dais, and the room seemed to be filled with strangers. The only people she knew were Helen Willis, looking strained and tense, and her husband, Bob.

Helen gave her testimony in a halting voice. Ruth Martin had come to stay with them early in the war, when so many children, and in some cases their mothers, had been evacuated from the cities and sent to places of safety. Mrs Martin had remained with them until she had gone to visit her mother in London; the old lady had been ill and Ruth had wanted to make sure that she was fully recovered. They later learned that the whole street had been destroyed in one of the bombing raids on the city and all the occupants in

Mrs Smith's house were presumed dead.

'So you kept the child, Lily, with you?' the female magistrate asked.

'Of course we did. What else were we supposed to do with her? She had nowhere else to go.'

'Quite. And when the war was over, did you inform the authorities that you still had charge of the child? Did you make any attempt to regularize the situation?'

'I don't know what you mean, my lady. I mean to say, everybody knew where she was. The billeting officer brought the two of them to us; there must be records somewhere about that.' Helen looked on anxiously as the magistrate turned to whisper something to her two companions on the bench.

'That will be all, Mrs Willis, thank you. You may be seated now. I call on Nurse Maude Rouse to give evidence, please.'

Maudie duly answered questions about the health and well-being of Lily Martin. Within minutes she was thanked for coming and dismissed. Was this all?

'I say!' she said, addressing the barrister

who was supposed to be representing the child. 'Aren't you going to say anything about that brother of Ruth Martin's? He tried to kidnap Lily and snatched Polly Willis instead. You can't send Lily back to a family like that! What sort of environment is that for a child?'

'This is not relevant,' the magistrate said. 'That will be all, Miss Rouse.'

'No! I must be allowed to speak! Are you aware that this child's uncle is a convicted murderer?'

'Silence! If you cannot control yourself, Miss Rouse, I shall have you removed!'

Fuming, Maudie sat down. She listened in growing dismay as the magistrate announced that she would discuss the case with her colleagues and would render their decision 'three weeks from today'. In the event that the child was to remain in England for the time being, the Willises would be investigated to ensure that they were fit and proper guardians for the minor child.

Later, Maudie waited outside the courthouse in case Helen and her husband needed support. 'Can you believe it!' Bob Willis roared. 'They're taking her into care while they look us over. They're sending a social worker to take her out of school this morning!'

'We're not allowed to see her in the meantime,' Helen sobbed. 'Anybody would think we're the criminals, not that Smith lot! Will you go to the school, Nurse, and try to explain things to her? She'll be that frightened.'

'No, I shan't have time,' Maudie said. 'I have other fish to fry.' Ignoring Helen's agonized squeak, she strode off down the street in the direction of the building that housed the offices of The *Chronicle*.

'Do you want the scoop of a lifetime?' Maudie demanded, facing the astonished reporter who had covered the church fête.

'Yes, of course. What is it?'

'It's about a local family who have been dogged by murder!' she replied. She was well aware that this was a wild exaggeration, and the resulting publicity might land her in Dick's bad books, but she had to take that chance if Lily was to be saved.

She went on to explain how Lily's

uncle — now a convicted killer — had kidnapped Polly by mistake, as a result of which Cyril Swain, Polly's paternal grandfather, had lost his life.

'But that's old hat!' the young man protested. 'That was before my time, but I remember reading about it in the dailies.'

'It may be old hat to you, but the prospect of a helpless child being shipped off to Australia to stay with a birth family that's unstable, to say the least, will stir the feelings of every female reader in the county. Play it up, man! Make a sob story out of it!'

'You'd have to convince my editor, Nurse Rouse, and I'm not sure he'd go for it. In fact, I know he wouldn't. Where's the angle, that's what he'll want to know.'

'Oh, I have an angle for you all right. The child's foster mother, Helen Willis, was the last person to see Madam Zora alive! What do you think of that, then?'

★　★　★

'You've done it now, Nurse Rouse!'
Maudie told herself as she sat in the bus,
being jogged back to Llandyfan. It was
one of those utilitarian buses where the
seats were made of polished wooden slats
rather than the more usual upholstered
ones of pre-war vintage. Each time the
bus hit a dip in the road the base of her
spine suffered.

That, however, was not the only
reason for her discomfort. In her
eagerness to help Lily, she had unfortunately let slip that she had seen the
murdered woman shortly before her
death, wearing Myrtle Blythe's cape. She
had recovered herself in time so that no
mention was made of her subsequent
conversations with Myrtle, but she would
be quoted in the newspaper just the
same. She could only hope that when the
reporter went to follow up on the story
with the victim's sister, no mention
would be made of Maudie's probing.

Nurses were not expected to get their
names in the papers, particularly when
murder was involved. She could only
hope that Dr Dean was too high-minded

to read the local rag.

In addition to whipping up public sympathy for Lily's plight, this article might result in something that would prove useful in the police investigation. Helen seemed to have total recall of the man she seen coming out of Madam Zora's tent. When interviewed, she would doubtless repeat all that, and the public would be alerted to trace the stranger.

★　★　★

On arriving at Llandyfan, Maudie hurried to the school, just in case Lily was there and in need of comforting. She learned that the little girl had already been taken away, 'without a word of warning' as the headmistress indignantly reported. 'Polly is still here, however, and in some distress. Perhaps you might like to see to her, Nurse?'

Polly was indeed very upset. 'I don't want the bad man to get her!' she sobbed.

'The bad man has gone, dear, and he won't be coming back,' Maudie explained, but the little girl continued to wail.

'There was a man! I saw him! He was driving the car when that lady came and took Lily away. I don't like it! I want my Mum! I want to go home!'

'And so you shall, dear,' Maudie said, frowning meaningfully at Miss Rice. 'I'll see her there myself if you've no objection.' The headmistress nodded her approval.

Helen flew to the door to greet them when they arrived, enfolding her daughter in her arms. 'The bad man's got Lily,' the little girl sobbed. 'I saw him, Mummy. He took her away in his car.'

Maudie put her finger to her lips to warn Helen to handle this carefully. It was obvious that Polly was still traumatized by her kidnapping the previous year and no doubt she had heard talk at school about the murder of Cyril Swain that had followed.

'Lily has gone to stay for a few days with that lady who came to the school to collect her,' Helen said. 'I expect she can't drive a car, so the man you saw was kindly giving them a lift.'

This must have sounded reasonable to Polly, for she calmed down at once. Few women drove cars, unless they'd learned the skill in the women's services during the war, and even now few ordinary families owned cars.

'When is Lily coming back, Mummy?'

'In a few days, pet. Now why don't you go upstairs and look at one of your books? I'll bring you a nice glass of pop in a few minutes.'

When the girl had trotted off, Helen turned to Maudie, biting her lip. 'I hate lying to the child, Nurse. I don't know what I'll do if they won't let us have Lily back.'

'Don't cross that bridge until you come to it,' Maudie advised. 'It may turn out for the best. Meanwhile, I should keep Polly home from school for a day or two. Miss Rice will understand. Children chatter so, and you don't want matters made worse if they come out with silly talk they've heard at home.'

★   ★   ★

The young reporter from The *Chronicle* did them proud. Maudie felt there wouldn't be a dry eye in the parish by the time people had finished reading the article. Helen Willis was represented as a traumatized mother suffering the effects of involvement with not one, but two murders, even though she hadn't been related to either victim or even seen the bodies. Maudie marvelled at what the writer had been able to concoct from very few facts and a lot of supposition.

Still, the results were startling. The following edition of the paper was full of letters to the editor, sent in by readers imploring the powers that be to let Lily stay in England with the family she knew and loved. Posters appeared in shop windows with such sentiments as 'Keep Lily Here! Don't Send Our Lily into Exile!'

Maudie was never to know whether this campaign did the trick, or even if the magistrates were made aware of it, but be that as it may the decision, when it was finally handed down three weeks later, was made in favour of the Willis family.

Lily was returned home to general rejoicing, to remain there until she turned sixteen, when she would be given the choice of staying in England or going to her birth mother in Australia.

A proviso was added that Lily and Ruth, her birth mother, should exchange letters from time to time. It wasn't fair to deprive a mother of her child entirely, the female magistrate said unctuously.

'I'll believe that when I see it,' Helen told Maudie. 'Until now our Lily hasn't heard a word from the woman since 1942 when she did her disappearing trick. Not a card on her birthday; not even a picture postcard with a koala bear on it or something.'

To Maudie's way of thinking the woman's real crime was that she'd let everyone believe she was dead when all the time she was very much alive. Fortunately Lily had been too young at the time to take it in properly, but Ruth could hardly expect to pop up years later, like a rabbit out of a hat, and expect everyone to fall on her neck.

29

Maudie loved her job, but she greatly disliked the paperwork that went with it. She didn't like the idea of carrying files with her when she went out to a case; it was hard enough carrying her medical bag on the bicycle without adding extra materials. Besides, patients' files were strictly confidential. It would be a disaster if ever they were dropped on the road or left in someone's home by mistake. Consequently, she jotted down a few hieroglyphics in a pocket notebook on the spot, and had to transfer them to her file cards whenever she had a spare moment.

She squinted at her notes. What on earth had Mrs Fowler's blood pressure been? The systolic reading was definitely 130, but the diastolic was unclear. It could be 70, or perhaps 78. Really, she must take the time to write more legibly! But when she had arrived at Betty Fowler's house the woman had been well advanced in labour, and Maudie had more to think about than beautiful handwriting.

The floor creaked as someone crossed the parish hall. She looked up and gasped. Framed in the doorway was a man, but not just any man. With his blue eyes and curly black hair, he could give Gregory Peck a run for his money any day. Who could he be? The husband of a prospective new patient, perhaps, come to register his wife with Maudie? Perhaps the long-awaited new curate for St John's? Close your mouth, Maudie! You'll swallow a fly.

'I hope I didn't startle you, Nurse,' the vision said, looking amused. He was probably used to this sort of reaction. He thrust out his hand. 'I'm Dr Lennox. Len Lennox, that is?'

'How do you do?'

'I've just arrived and I thought I'd better pop in and introduce myself, seeing as we'll be working together.'

'We will?'

'I certainly hope so. Has nobody told you? I'm the other half of Dr Mallory's old practice. I've just bought a half share.'

'Nobody mentioned it,' Maudie murmured. 'But then Dr Dean doesn't seem to think that explanations are necessary. He just barks out orders and when he says 'jump' I'm supposed to ask, 'How high?''

He laughed. 'Oh, you mustn't mind old Don! He can be a bit snooty at times, but he's a sound man medically.'

'Except that he was standing behind the door when the bedside manners were given out,' Maudie mused, but she managed to bite her tongue before sharing this thought with the newcomer. He seemed like a friendly young man, but he was an unknown quantity and she mustn't get on the wrong side of him right from the start.

'We haven't sorted out all the details yet,' Lennox said, 'but we're planning to divide up the district between us. We were classmates in med school, you see, and we know each other's strengths and weaknesses. For the moment I'll be dealing with the Llandyfan district and I hope you'll set me on the right path. Fill me in on the woes of the various patients and all that.'

'Where will the two of you be living?' Maudie asked, not quite willing to accept the situation yet. Her cottage was small and she couldn't quite see two large men bumbling around in it without encountering difficulties.

'Oh, Don is taking over Mallory's house. The old Doc is going to live with his sister at Weston-Super-Mare. I'm afraid Don had visions of a lovely new clinic, stocked with all the latest gadgets, but that will have to wait until the housing crisis is well and truly over. He'll see patients in those downstairs rooms that Doc Mallory has used for his surgery since Noah was a boy.'

'And what about you? Have you found a place for yourself yet?'

'Ah, now that's why I've chosen to come to Llandyfan, you see. I'll be bunking in with my aunt.'

'Your aunt!'

'Yes, Mrs Beasley, my mother's sister. Do you know her?'

Maudie had met the lady at Mothers'

Union meetings but had never attended her as a nurse. Mrs Beasley had a rambling old house some two miles outside the village, surrounded by extensive grounds. 'Auntie says she'll be glad to have me. She's fed up with rattling around in that great place all alone and she wants me there to frighten off prospective burglars.' He laughed again.

Maudie felt as though a great weight had been lifted off her shoulders. 'What will you do about a surgery? Dr Dean mentioned something about renovating the parish hall, but I don't think the vicar is too keen.'

'Oh, no problem there. I'm going to do up the old gatehouse on the estate. It will be just the ticket. There's two rooms and a scullery downstairs. The troops can have one for a waiting room, and I'll do my magic in the other. I'm getting the phone installed today. What could be better?'

What indeed? 'It will be a long way for some of the patients to walk, though,' she suggested.

'Good for them! People these days

don't get enough exercise, Nurse. Besides, I'll be doing house calls so the really sick won't have to walk anywhere.'

When the doctor had left, promising to return in due course to discuss strategy, Maudie sat at her desk in a daze, overjoyed at the change in circumstances. When Mrs Blunt came in some fifteen minutes later, she found her friend singing at the top of her lungs: *'O, Praise Him! Alleluia! Alleluia!'*

'You sound cheerful, Nurse. If you carry on like this we'll have to find you a place in the church choir!'

'Oops! I didn't hear you coming!'

'I should jolly well think you couldn't, bellowing like that. I take it you've heard the news, then.'

'Yes, the new doctor called in earlier. Did you know about this? Why didn't you let me know?'

'We had some idea, but I didn't want to get your hopes up until it was certain. I know how worried you've been. Cora Beasley has been angling for this a long time. She's a widow, of course, and I know she's been so lonely since her son was killed at El Alamein. It will do her good to have some young company in the house.

'This is for your ears only, Nurse, — if you haven't deafened yourself with that singing — but I happen to know that she helped him to buy his share of Dr Mallory's practice. Her husband left her quite well fixed, but her sister's family isn't nearly so well off, and young Leonard probably wouldn't have been able to raise the money himself.'

'That's very generous of her.'

'Well, she is something of a parish benefactress, you know. Besides, as she said, it will do the boy more good to get the benefit of her money now than wait until after she's dead and buried. So what did you think of him, Nurse?'

'He seems pleasant enough, but I'm afraid he's a bit of a heart throb! All the teenagers will have their heads turned, I'm sure. Greta Black may even forget about her precious film stars when she sees the real thing on the village street!'

'If I were twenty-five years younger I could fancy him myself,' Mrs Blunt said, with a wicked grin. 'No, better make that thirty years!'

'And you a married woman, and a vicar's wife at that!'

'There's no harm in looking, as I told young Billy Mayer after Mrs Hatch caught him stealing a sherbet dab last week. It's when thoughts turn to actions that the trouble starts.'

'Speaking of which, I really should be getting on with these files,' Maudie sighed. 'But I can't seem to settle down to it now. I feel like celebrating! You wouldn't like to come to the Copper Kettle with me, I suppose? I could murder a Chelsea bun.'

'Get thee behind me, Satan! Those things always go straight to my hips. A cup of coffee and a scone shouldn't hurt, though.'

'Nonsense! This calls for a splurge! Éclairs and Napoleons, here we come!'

Maudie locked up her office and the two women strolled out into the sunshine.

30

Miss Rice rang Maudie. 'Could you possibly pop over to the school, Nurse? We have a little boy here who isn't at all well.'

'Yes, I'll come at once. What seems to be the matter?'

'He seems to be burning up, and he has a runny nose. I do think we'll have to send him home, but he shouldn't be allowed out in this state, and his parents aren't on the phone.'

'Who is it?'

'Young Danny Harper.'

'Oh, yes, we know each other well. His house is only a mile from the school so he should be able to manage the walk, poor little mite. I'll see him home myself.'

'Thank you, Nurse. I'll see you in a few minutes, then.'

Danny's mother received him with cries of concern. 'He was all right at breakfast time, Nurse, or I never would have let him go to school today.'

'That's children for you,' Maudie remarked. 'Racing about one minute and coming down with something the next. Still, they usually bounce back just as easily. Danny is running a temperature, so you should put him to bed and give him plenty of fluids. If you see no improvement in a day or two I'll ask the doctor to call round. Or you can call me at once if you happen to see anything that worries you.'

'Oh, I don't want that doctor!' Mrs Harper sniffed.

'Why not? It's all free now, you know.'

'I don't care if it comes with free nylons and a box of Turkish delight! I'm not letting that man over my doorstep!'

Maudie was interested to know that she wasn't the only one to have fallen afoul of Dr Dean. 'You've had dealings with him before, then? I wasn't aware of that.'

Mrs Harper pulled a face. 'I met him in the shop the other day when I went there to fetch an ounce of baccy for my hubby. 'This is our new doctor,' says Mrs Hatch. Well, I wanted to make him feel

269

welcome-like, so I said I was ever so glad we'd got a new doctor at last, because my bunion is acting up something fierce. 'My good woman,' he tells me, 'if you wish to consult me on a professional basis you must telephone for an appointment. My time is too valuable to waste on giving free advice to all and sundry in shops.' The cheek of it, Nurse! I ask you!'

Maudie could sympathize with the doctor in a way. Doctors were always being asked for free advice when in ordinary social situations. It was only right that patients should go through the proper channels, and only fair that doctors should be paid for their expertise. However, the man had no need to be so rude.

'Perhaps you didn't know that we've got a different doctor now. He's a Dr Lennox and from what I've seen of him he's a lovely man. I'm sure the children will love him.' Not to mention the ladies of this parish! she added silently.

'Lennox? I've never met that name round here before.'

'He's not a local lad, but he's no

stranger, either. He's Mrs Beasley's nephew.

'Well, I never!'

Having seen Danny safely installed in bed with a glass of Corona at his side, Maudie prepared to leave.

'Will you be going past the Royal Oak on your way home, Nurse?' his mother asked.

'Yes, I can easily go round that way. What did you have in mind?'

'I borrowed a crochet pattern from Bill's stepmother and I promised to let her have it back today. The trouble is, I'll be stuck indoors now, with Danny like this.'

'I'll be glad to hand it in to Mrs Frost for you. What are you making with it?'

'I thought I was going to do a doily, but it's too complicated for me. I'm going to try folding paper and cutting out shapes instead. You can't go wrong with that.'

'And speaking for myself, I'd rather put a paper one underneath a cake anyway,' Maude observed. 'I've tried getting icing off a cotton doily and it's a miserable job.

The stuff always gets in between the stitches and won't come out.'

* * *

When Maudie neared the Royal Oak, she saw a small group of men going in. Dick was among them. While he was smartly dressed in uniform, the others were in plain clothes, which she correctly understood to mean that they were police detectives. 'Probably still looking into the murder,' she muttered. They had probably brought Dick along to show them what was what, since they were outsiders who didn't know the country, or its people.

She loitered about for a few minutes before going in, in case Dick got the idea that she was infringing on his territory. Amateur sleuth as she was, she wouldn't want his superiors to think that Dick was giving away too much to his lady friend. At last she attached herself to a group of elderly men whose habit it was to visit the pub at lunchtime.

She found the landlord's wife busily

distributing plates of appetizing-looking sandwiches. 'I've come to return this pattern from Mrs Harper,' she said, holding out the pamphlet in question.

'Oh, that thing! You might as well put it in the bin. I'm that fed up with it. It looks so pretty in the pattern, don't it, but it's that awkward to make. And the thread is so fine! My eyes isn't what they was, neither.'

Sid the pot man acknowledged Maudie's presence with a lopsided salute. 'Come to see the old trout upstairs, have you?'

'If you mean Miss Blythe, the answer is no, I haven't. I just popped in for a moment to see Mrs Frost.'

'Just as well, then, because she's already got another visitor.'

'Well, it's a free country. I expect it's a lady friend.'

'That's where you'd be wrong, then. It's a man, see. That foreign chap in the fancy dress.'

Maudie interpreted this to mean a man in outlandish garments rather than a woman's frock! And then she realized what Sid had said. Wilbur Brownlow!

'Aye, and he's been round these parts before.' This was contributed by one of the locals propping up the bar. 'Remember the day the old duck fell in the drink and we had to fish her out? That same chap was there then.'

'Say that again?' Maudie said, puzzled.

'Me and my mates were scraping down our old boat at the time. It needed a bit of caulking and painting, see? This bloke had a houseboat moored upstream a bit from our boathouse. On holiday, he said he was. Staying with his wife.'

'And this man is upstairs with Miss Blythe now?' Maudie demanded.

'That's what I said, didn't I?' Sid sounded indignant. 'You women is all the same. You never listen to a chap.'

Maudie ignored him. Waving frantically, she tried to catch Dick's eye. He excused himself and walked over to her, not moving quickly enough for her liking.

'Sorry, Maudie. As you can see, I'm a bit busy at the moment. I'll get back to you later.'

'It's Brownlow!' she hissed. 'He's up

there now with poor Miss Blythe. You've got to do something, Dick, before it's too late!'

Things moved quickly after that. The police stampeded up the stairs, having ordered two of the locals to block the exit from the outside door leading to the guest rooms. Maudie scrambled after the official party, only to be rebuffed at the head of the stairs. Unwillingly she joined the onlookers outside. She did not have long to wait.

Brownlow, still wearing his cream-coloured suit, was hustled out in handcuffs. The detectives, who had apparently arrived in two different cars, climbed into their vehicles. Dick appeared at the door.

'You can come up now, Nurse. Miss Blythe needs you.'

'He tried to strangle me, Nurse!' Miss Blythe cried, rubbing her neck. 'He tried to kill me with his bare hands! And before you ask, I am not talking about something that happened in one of my past lives. That skunk is my brother-in-law and he killed my sister. Now he's tried to dispose of me!' Who was it who said that imminent death concentrates the mind wonderfully, or something along those lines? It was obvious to Maudie that Miss Blythe was very much in her right mind at this moment. Her narrow escape had jerked her firmly into the twentieth century.

★ ★ ★

Later that day, Dick turned up at Maudie's cottage, where she'd been waiting in a fever of impatience. 'How is Miss Blythe?' he asked, even before she had shut the door behind him.

'She's safely tucked up in the cottage hospital. She didn't want to go, but Dr Lennox insisted. He delivered her there in his own car just to be sure she'd do as she's told. But what about Brownlow? Have you managed to get anything out of him?'

'Wilbur Brownlow, alias Hiram Green. He's well known to the police in New York as a high-flying gambler.'

'Imagine! Was he really married to Madam Zora? Did he kill her? And if so, why? And why did he try to kill Myrtle Blythe?'

'Whoa! One question at a time! Let's wait until we're sitting down, and I'll tell you what I know, but please don't go blabbing it about until we've prepared our case.'

'Dick Bryant, I don't blab, as you put it. And may I remind you that if it wasn't for me, you fellows wouldn't have gone up there in time to save Miss Blythe from a sticky end!'

Maudie poured hot water into the teapot and swirled it about, looking aggrieved. Dick got the message. 'Sorry, Miss Marple! But you do see how careful we have to be? If anything gets out that might weaken our case, Brownlow might get off. At least he's singing like a canary at the moment, which gives us a good start.'

When the tea was made and Maudie had dug out some ginger nuts to go with it, she looked at Dick expectantly. 'Well, what are we waiting for?'

'Yes,' he said. 'Brownlow was legally married to Madam Zora — Octavia

Blythe. According to her sister, who has already been interviewed again by Detective Inspector Groom, they met on a cruise and were married on board by the captain. Octavia was giving some sort of psychic consultations there and we suspect that Wilbur was honing his skills as a card sharp.'

'I see.'

'So they eventually ended up back in the United States, where Wilbur did poorly at the gaming tables and lost heavily. He fell into the hands of money lenders and when he couldn't pay up they threatened to put cement boots on him and drop him off the end of a pier.'

'Ouch!'

'So Wilbur must have thought that his wife's sister was the answer to all his prayers. The couple came to England hoping to appeal to Myrtle's better nature. Blood is thicker than water, and all that. But as the old girl told you, Maudie, she had suffered quite enough over the years at the hands of her half-sister and she saw no reason why she should bail her out now.'

'And what was all that I heard about a houseboat, moored on the river? A bit of a comedown after a cruise ship, wasn't it?'

'That was quite true. They wanted to stay out of sight of any nosy parkers who might connect them with any mayhem that resulted, yet be close enough to the Royal Oak so they could keep the sister in view.'

'Oh! So was it true, then, about Miss Blythe being pushed into the river that day?'

'Brownlow says not. He maintains that they were simply renewing their efforts to make her pay up and she got frightened and ran away from them, slipping in the process.'

'It's hard to know who is telling the truth,' Maudie observed. 'Not that it matters, now you have the man in custody.'

'Except that his wife is dead.'

'And did he kill her, do you think? To me, it doesn't add up. It would have made more sense to kill Myrtle, in the hope that all her money would go to Octavia, as next of kin. And what about Myrtle's cape? I still don't understand what that had to do with anything.'

'If you believe what Myrtle told the inspector, she lent the garment to her sister to cover up her costume so the punters wouldn't notice her, which is exactly what she told you.'

'Yes, but if Wilbur was the murderer he couldn't possibly confuse the two women. So why kill her?'

'According to his own testimony, the man says he didn't mean to kill her. Myrtle had promised to pay Octavia something for doing her Madam Zora act in aid of the church, and he followed his wife into the tent to find out how much it was going to be. The sum turned out to be far less than he had hoped, and it was certainly not sufficient to square his debt with the loan sharks. He gave her a punch — to teach her a lesson, he says — and she fell, hitting her head on the sharp corner of the metal table. Forensics say it was that blow to the temple that killed her.'

'But she was stabbed!'

'Yes, but not fatally. The silly fool rammed the knife into her, hoping to deflect suspicion from himself. When the scout reported his knife missing we'd get the idea that some local villain had picked it up, using it to attack the fortune-teller in a botched robbery. Mrs Willis's testimony was useful there, both in narrowing down the time of death and proving that Brownlow was in the vicinity when the murder was committed.'

'Ad then I suppose he had to keep trying to worm money out of Myrtle Blythe, so he could get away. But what good would it do him to kill her? I don't suppose she had thousands of pounds in bank notes lying around her room.'

Dick shrugged. 'He says he was making one last effort to convince her to part with the cash, she haughtily refused him, and he lost his temper and started to shake her. If we hadn't burst in when we did he would have let her go again unscathed.'

'A likely story!'

'Yes, well, it's all over now. What happens next is for a jury to decide.'

'I'm not so sure we've heard the last of Miss Myrtle Blythe, though,' Maudie said. 'As far as I'm concerned she's a sort of female Mad Hatter. Who knows where she'll pop up next?'

Dick raised his eyebrows. 'Any more tea in that pot? All this talking has left me parched.'

31

The nights were drawing in. The inhabitants of Llandyfan had given up their evening walks along the riverbank and their gardens had been put to bed for the winter. Salad lunches had been replaced by comfort foods such as macaroni cheese or steak and kidney pudding. The various social activities, such as the Girl Guides and the vestry meetings, had resumed for the season. In short, Llandyfan was settling in for the coming winter.

On this November evening a visitor from outer space, peeping into Maudie's cottage, might well have assumed that here were a married couple, the day's work done, contentedly spending a quiet evening together before bedtime.

Dick Bryant was sitting beside the fire, quietly smoking his pipe and listening to the music of Victor Sylvester on the wireless. Maudie sat closer to the ring of light shed by a standard lamp; she was crocheting a lacy edging onto the end of a plain pillowcase.

'Making that for your bottom drawer, are you?' Dick said suddenly.

'Good gracious, no!' Maudie said with a rueful laugh. 'I'm afraid I'm a bit long in the tooth to bother with a bottom drawer. I'm just a bit fed up with plain old sheets and pillowcases. Everything in the shops nowadays is what they call utility, meaning just that: useful, but nothing to write home about. I thought I'd take up fancywork again and have a go at beautifying my surroundings.'

'You beautify your surroundings just by being here,' Dick said in a low voice.

'Dick Bryant! What sort of nonsense is that?'

'I mean it, Maudie. Look around you. Everything here is the result of your handiwork. The antimacassars on the sofa, the pretty picture on that wall, the rug you hooked years ago, even the biscuits in the caddy. You baked those. You have a talent for homemaking, gal.'

'It's nice of you to say so, Dick. I do

what I can to keep the place nice.'

'I'm not putting this very well. Yes, you've made things nice here but what I'm trying to say is that it's you, Maudie. You being here is what makes the place special.'

'What on earth brought this on, Dick?'

He shuffled his feet in their plaid carpet slippers, wrinkling the hearthrug. 'Oh, I don't know. I've felt this coming on for a long time, and now I can't keep it in any longer. I think I love you, Maudie.'

Maudie's hand flew to her mouth. What was the world coming to? Good old Dick Bryant, talking about love! She became aware that he was looking at her anxiously. 'Well, now,' she said.

'So what I was wondering was . . . '

'Yes? What were you wondering, Dick?'

'Could you ever feel the same about me?'

She thought for a moment. 'Yes, Dick. I can honestly say that I love you, too.'

'That's all right then,' he said, beaming at her. He leaned back in his armchair, drawing on his pipe.

Maudie set her sewing aside. Yes, she

had come to love Dick Bryant, but was she *in* love? It was hard to know. She enjoyed the time they spent together. She wanted the best for him in all ways; you did when you loved someone. What if something happened to him? What if he if he went away and found somebody else and she no longer had any claim on him? Would she grieve? She knew then that the bottom would fall out of her world. Maudie Rouse, midwife, forty-three years of age, was in love. How could she have missed the signs?

What about all those times when she had dressed to attract him, cooked meals to delight him, thought up outings that he might enjoy? She had not consciously been trying to snare him! No, it was in her nature to do kind things for people. Why else had she become a nurse if it were not so? However, she had fallen into a comfortable relationship with Dick Bryant, and now she wondered where it was leading.

Dick noticed her staring at him. 'Do you mind if I switch off the wireless?' he said.

'I suppose it's all right. Aren't you enjoying the programme?'

'It's not that. I want to say something, Maudie.'

'I thought you just did.'

Victor Sylvester's band was shut off abruptly. Dick stood up and began to pace back and forth in front of the fireplace.

'Come on, Dick,' Maudie said, looking at the clock. 'It's almost time for your bus.'

'Forget the bus! Look here, Maudie, I think we should get married. What do you say about that?'

'Married!' she squeaked, playing for time. Dick sank down on his knees in front of her.

'I know I'm not much good with words,' he went on. 'In fact, I expect I'm doing this all wrong. I know women need a bit of romance, like you see on the pictures. The trouble is I don't know where to find a gypsy violinist, and I couldn't even bring you flowers. There's nothing much available in November.'

'No, no, there isn't.'

'But I do love you and I want to spend the rest of my life with you. So what do you say, Maudie? Will you have me?'

'Oh Dick! I don't know what to say!'

'Can't you say yes?' he pleaded.

Maudie took his face in her work-worn hands. 'I'll need time to think, Dick. I do love you, and if I thought about marrying anyone it would certainly be you.'

'Then what's the difficulty? We're both free agents. I earn enough to support a wife; not in any great style, I admit, but as the good book says, better a dinner of herbs where love is, than a stalled ox and hatred therewith.'

'Oh, money isn't everything.'

'My sentiments exactly. I'd like to give you the world, Maudie, but if that's not possible I'll do my best to make you feel safe and secure. I'd never do anything to hurt you. What I'm offering is my total love and devotion.'

Tears sprang to Maudie's eyes. Who would have thought that Dick Bryant could be so poetic? 'I know you would, Dick, but the problem may be with me. I'm forty-three years old.'

'So what? I'm forty-five.'

'I'm set in my ways. I've lived alone for so long that I have my own way of doing things. I enjoy my independence. I can't promise to adapt to another person's style of living. If I'd married in my twenties, or if I was a widow now, it would be very different. And there's another thing! I'm too old to have children. If you married me you'd never have the chance to be a father.'

Dick shrugged. 'Perhaps that was never on the cards for me. And if I fathered children now I'd be drawing my pension before they were off our hands. Besides, who would want to bring children into this world? I lost so many of my friends in that beastly war, Maudie. How do you think it would it feel to bring up sons, only to see them wiped out on some horrible battlefield if we have another war?'

'Heaven forbid,' Maudie whispered. She now how a good idea why Dick had given away his beloved train set to little Ambrose, who was equally a victim of war.

'Oh!' Dick muttered, looking aghast. 'I wasn't thinking. It's your job to bring children into the world. I hope you didn't think I was criticizing you, Maudie. I truly didn't mean to give offense.'

'None taken.' She grinned. 'Anyway, I just assist when the babies are ready to come out of the womb. I'm not responsible for putting them there in the first place!'

They were silent for a while, each of them with their own memories. Then, glancing at his wristwatch, Dick shot to his feet. 'Good grief, look at the time! I'll have to get going soon, unless I want to foot it all the way to Midvale! Listen, I can see you need time to think, old girl, but can't you give me any hope at all, just to be going on with?'

Standing up, Maudie took a deep breath. 'I'd love to be your wife, Dick, but . . .'

He swept her into his arms and she felt his lips on hers. This was not one of the sweet kisses he had bestowed on her in the past, but something stronger, more urgent. She felt as if she was melting into his embrace, leaving the world behind with all its cares. 'I wish you didn't have to go,' she whispered, when he finally released her.

'So do I, but I'll be back! We'll talk again, Maudie, and try to iron out all your worries. I know I can convince you that we're doing the right thing. But for now, though, you have agreed to be my wife; isn't that right?' He regarded her anxiously, as if he feared she might change her mind.

'Yes, I have,' Maudie said firmly.

Left alone beside the dying fire, Maudie was amazed at what had just taken place. Dick had asked her to marry him. Even more amazing, she had agreed! Was she doing the right thing?

Yes, she loved Dick. She wanted to be with him for the rest of her life. No more saying goodbye on the doorstep as he dashed off to catch the last bus to Midvale. Instead, waving him goodbye when he left for work in the morning, and being there to greet him when he returned home at the end of the day.

There were other advantages to marriage, too. While motherhood was not on the cards for her, she would have a husband to look after, in good times and bad. There would always be someone to share her anxieties with, and to recount the happenings of the day. She would listen with interest while Dick told her of the events of his daily round.

A little voice in her head asked her if she wasn't being too romantic? Thinking of some of the husbands she knew, she wondered how their wives put up with them. Paul Allen, Frank Black, Graham Davis! Had their wives gone into marriage with stars in their eyes, only to be disillusioned later? Had those men presented a very different face during their courting days, only to revert to their true selves later? Could that happen with Dick Bryant?

No! Maudie silenced the nasty little voice. He was open and honest. He might well turn out to have some irritating little habits, but which of us does not? She thought uncomfortably about that silly magazine article, which had pointed out her own flaws. She would need to make a few changes there, if she hoped to live up to Dick's expectations.

Yes, she had doubts, but surely every prospective bride had those. A bride! She was going to be a bride, at her age! A host of new questions flooded her mind. Where would the wedding take place? St John's, of course. June was the best month for weddings, which would give her time to sort everything out.

And what would she wear? Regretfully, she set aside the notion of herself as a bride, which she'd had since she was very young. Not for Nurse Maudie Rouse the lacy white gown or the coronet of daisies on her head. She wouldn't wear anything that would be useful later on, though. For once she would splurge on something that would make her look beautiful for Dick. She had better start saving her clothing coupons right away.

The embers of the fire disintegrated into ashes, but Maudie, wrapped around in a rosy glow, had no sense that the room was becoming cold. It was hard to believe, but in 1949 she would become Mrs Dick Bryant. Turning off the lamp, she went upstairs to bed. Heaven was in her hand.

32

It was a cold November morning. On her way to the parish hall, Maudie found herself shivering. She should have put a cardigan on under her Burberry, but misled by the cosy atmosphere of her cottage she hadn't bothered. She was sorry now. There wasn't much warmth in the short-sleeved cotton frock.

She glanced up at the leaden sky. She hoped that a storm wasn't on its way. She had only one expectant mother on her list, and that was Mrs Barden, who wasn't due for another two weeks. However, as Maudie knew of old, babies often took it into their heads to rush into the world at the first sign of bad weather, whether it was winter snow or summer thunder and lightning. Why should Baby Barden be the exception?

Mrs Barden lived at the far end of the parish, which meant that Maudie would arrive soaking wet after cycling through a downpour. If the worst happened and snow came, she could foresee herself trudging through slush, wheeling her machine. She sighed. She loved her job, but she did wish that babies could be born on sunny mornings rather than dark nights. A little voice in her mind suggested that if she married Dick Bryant, she would never have to turn out in nasty weather again, or at least not in connection with her work.

Stepping into the parish hall, she met Mrs Blunt coming out. The other woman's eyes lit up when she saw Maudie.

'Oh, Nurse! Isn't it wonderful? I was so delighted to hear the news, and of course you must be even more so!'

'What!' How had the news got out so fast? Hadn't she and Dick agreed to keep their own counsel until something more definite was on the cards? 'How did you hear about it?'

Mrs Blunt gave her a funny look. 'Why, it was on the wireless this morning! Didn't you hear it?'

'Er, no. I didn't have the wireless on.

What are you talking about? And why must I be delighted?'

'It's Princess Elizabeth, Nurse. She's had a little boy!'

'Oh! Oh, I see.'

'A little prince! Just think, he'll be king of England some day. Not that I shall live to see it. And I knew you'd be interested because delivering babies is your life, isn't it, Nurse? Don't you wish you could have been there, to take part in it all?'

'I expect the baby was delivered by doctors. They can't take chances with royalty.'

Yes, it was a great event, but Maudie certainly would not have wanted the responsibility. She knew she was good at her job, but nothing was ever certain when it came to delivering babies.

'I wonder what they'll call him?' Mrs Blunt went on. 'George, perhaps, for his grandfather, or Philip, after his own papa?' She broke off to blink at Maudie. 'You thought I was referring to something else, didn't you? Now what could that have been?'

'I was thinking I should have put on a

cardi and wondering if I should slip home to fetch one.'

Mrs Blunt's face lit up with a smile. 'I know what it is, Nurse Rouse! You have some news of your own, haven't you? Is there something you'd like to tell me?'

Maudie blushed. 'Nothing's been decided yet, Mrs Blunt.'

'Well, do come to see Harold as soon as you have something definite to share. We have a lot of weddings at St John's and you'll want your pick of suitable dates. And may I say, Nurse, that I believe you and Constable Bryant will make a very suitable couple.' Mrs Blunt smirked.

THE END

We do hope that you have enjoyed reading this large print book.

Did you know that all of our titles are available for purchase?

We publish a wide range of high quality large print books including:
Romances, Mysteries, Classics
General Fiction
Non Fiction and Westerns

Special interest titles available in large print are:
The Little Oxford Dictionary
Music Book, Song Book
Hymn Book, Service Book

Also available from us courtesy of Oxford University Press:
Young Readers' Dictionary
(large print edition)
Young Readers' Thesaurus
(large print edition)

For further information or a free brochure, please contact us at:
Ulverscroft Large Print Books Ltd.,
The Green, Bradgate Road, Anstey,
Leicester, LE7 7FU, England.
Tel: (00 44) 0116 236 4325
Fax: (00 44) 0116 234 0205